The OTHER *Sister*

ALSO BY S.T. UNDERDAHL

Remember This

S.T. Underdahl

The OTHER Sister

flux™

Woodbury, Minnesota

First Edition
Third Printing, 2008

Book design by Steffani Chambers
Cover design by Ellen Dahl
Cover photograph © 2006 Charles Gullung / Photonica / Getty Images
Editing by Rhiannon Ross

Flux, an imprint of Llewellyn Publications

The Cataloging-in-Publication Data for *The Other Sister* is on file at the Library of Congress.

   ISBN-13: 978-0-7387-0933-8
   ISBN-10: 0-7387-0933-6

Flux
A Division of Llewellyn Worldwide, Ltd.
2143 Wooddale Drive, Dept. 978-0-7387-0933-8
Woodbury, MN 55125-2989, U.S.A.
www.fluxnow.com

Printed in the United States of America

Acknowledgments

I would like to thank the wonderful people at Flux: Andrew Karre, Rhiannon Ross, Kelly Hailstone, Steffani Chambers, and Ellen Dahl. You do great work, and I thank you from the bottom of my heart for making the publication of my first book such an enjoyable and rewarding experience.

Thank you to my beloved friends and family; your support means the world to me and neither I, nor *The Other Sister*, would exist without it. Extra-special thanks to Tonja Rystad, Shirley Tyler, and to my W.O.W. Sisters: Joanne, Bethann, Margo, Rita, and the Michelles for their friendship and interest in this project.

Finally, thanks to my wonderful husband, Shane, and to the greatest kids in the world, Navy, Fiona, Beck, Alexa, Chloe, and Jaiden, all of whom inspire me every day. I am truly blessed.

For my family, in all its amazing forms.

1

When I became a teenager, it finally occurred to me that life is a lot like one of those water-filled snow globes. You know the type; the little scene inside is tranquil and serene until someone comes along and gives it a shake, and suddenly that peaceful world becomes chaos. That's pretty much what happened to me on Thursday, October 1st, the day I found out that everything I'd ever believed about my life, my family, and especially my parents, was a big fat *lie*. Or maybe I should say that the whole thing began on a sunny day in August, ten years before I was even born. But that would be jumping ahead . . .

I'd spent the evening studying with my best friends, Sarah and Britt, for the next day's psychology test. We always study together at one of our houses, where we split a big bag of Doritos and drink Diet Coke with lots of ice.

After we finish the Doritos, we break out the M&Ms; I pick out the brown ones, Sarah likes the green ones, and Britt eats all the rest. We usually end up feeling sick, but it's a system that works; Sarah and I always get As. Britt, on the other hand, usually gets stuck with a B.

"I don't know why it is," she grumbled to us after the last test in American Government. "We study exactly the same stuff."

"Maybe *you're* spending too much time studying the *Howler* for pictures of Brandon Burke," Sarah teased.

Britt made an indignant face at her. "We *all* do that," she pointed out.

"I'm able to prioritize and divide my time between my studies and my other interests," Sarah replied primly, then broke into a grin at Britt's scowl. "Like lusting after Brandon Burke."

"Alright you two," I said, watching Sarah deflect the punch that Britt had aimed at her shoulder. "Britt, next time we'll just have to work harder to make sure you've really got the material down."

"Hmmph." She tossed her wavy red hair. "All I can say is that it's a good thing that Brandon Burke is more interested in beauty than in brains."

Sarah and I traded looks. "What exactly are you saying?" Sarah challenged.

Britt ignored the question, and struck a pose. "How does this sound to you guys?" she intoned dreamily. "*Brandon and Brittany Burke* . . . don't you just love the sound of it?" Britt pretended to stare off into space, "And we'll name our children . . . oh, let's see . . . *Bethany* and *Blake*. Or maybe *Beyoncé* and *Benjamin*. Can't you just picture the Christmas card?"

She looked at us out of the corner of her eye, and a moment later we all burst into laughter. The truth was, none of us had a chance with Brandon Burke, and we all darn well knew it. He was the most popular boy in the junior class, a star on the cross-country team, and the best-looking boy imaginable with his silky golden hair and the sort of skin that flushed to a deep ruddiness when he came in from the outdoors.

"He's so *pretty*," Sarah had sighed more than once. "Like Prince William." No one argued with her on that one.

Compared to Brandon Burke, we were essentially invisible. I'm not saying we're complete freaks, but we were only sophomores and basically not even in the same stratosphere. Of all of us, Britt probably did have the best chance, with her cute figure, sparkling brown eyes, and pretty, full lips that boys always stared at when she talked.

If I had to say, I'd probably describe myself as average looking; not really striking, like Britt, but not scary either. My eyes are green and my hair is sandy blond, like my dad's, although mine's long and he likes to point out how he's losing his. Sarah and Britt claim that I look a lot like Sarah Michelle Gellar from *Buffy the Vampire Slayer*, but I think they're just trying to be nice. My dad says I remind him of Barbara Eden from the old TV show *I Dream of*

Jeannie. I've seen it a few times on Nick at Nite, and I guess I can see what he means.

Sarah is fine-featured and brunette, but her glasses and the ever-present headband make her look serious and bookish, kind of like a young Hillary Clinton. Not surprisingly, she plans to go to law school.

"Hey, Sarah, what do you get when you cross a lying politician and a crooked lawyer?" my brother, Jake, asked her one day when we were studying at our house. For some reason, Jake seems to take particular pleasure in teasing Sarah.

She looked up from her algebra, her face pink. "I don't know, what?"

"Chelsea Clinton!" Jake crowed, clearly enjoying her look of annoyance. As he sauntered out of the room she aimed her most scornful insult at his retreating back.

"Republican!"

While Sarah wants to be a lawyer, I, on the other hand, have planned to be a psychologist ever since I can remember. I can picture myself sitting in a big office with a nice desk and my diplomas on the wall. I'll have really comfortable leather chairs where people can sit and tell me their problems, to which I will murmur, "Mm-hmm, tell me more . . ." or "How did you feel about that?"

I secretly think I have potential to be a very good psychologist, because it already seems like people tend to tell me their problems. Sometimes when I'm listening I let myself imagine that I'm really a therapist listening to my patient. I make a point to show them that I really understand what they're going through. When you know what you want to do with your life, it's a good idea to take every available opportunity to practice.

That's why I wasn't particularly worried about the next day's test in psychology. Our teacher, Mrs. Gasparini, knew I had a special interest in the subject, and had already been giving me extra reading. Jake was in her class when he was a sophomore, and she was always joking that he should be the subject of a research paper. It wasn't *really* a joke, as far as I was concerned, because my older brother is nuttier than a candy bar. Ever since he took Intro to Spanish in the eighth grade Jake has been completely obsessed. And I don't just mean that he finds Spanish culture interesting; Jake wants to *be* Latino. It's the most obnoxious thing you've ever seen; any conversation with him is peppered with Spanish words, and it's gotten to the point that he even speaks English with a Spanish accent. Since Language Arts is a requirement in our school, I can usually understand most of what he's saying, but it's highly annoying, all the same. My parents think Jake's weird obsession is hilarious, and call him "Juan Taco," which obviously only encourages him. It probably shouldn't come as a surprise, either, if I told you that Jake's girlfriend, Lilja, is Chicana. She still has lots of family in Mexico, so naturally Jake plans to move there as soon as he graduates. As you can see, the whole thing is ridiculous, and sometimes I think he does it just to get on my nerves.

Anyway, after we wrapped up studying and cleaned up our crumbs, Sarah's dad drove me and Britt home. When I got inside, I hung my coat in the closet and left my book bag by the back door. I know my dad hates it when we pile things by the back door for him to trip over in the morning, but the way I see it, there's no point carrying stuff all the way up to my room only to carry it back down again in the morning.

I could hear the television set going in the family room, and guessed that my mom was probably in there, curled up as usual in her recliner with the daily crossword puzzle. When I stuck my head in the door to say goodnight, however, I was surprised to find the television was playing to an empty room. A moment later I bumped right into Mom as I passed through the darkened kitchen on my way upstairs.

"Oh, Josey! You startled me!" she exclaimed, clutching her chest. I was pleased to see she was wearing the soft yellow pajamas I'd given her for Christmas last year.

"Sorry if I scared you," I apologized. "No one was around so I thought you all must've gone to bed early."

"No," she smiled at me in the semi-darkness, reaching over to flip on the kitchen light. "Your dad went to bed and the boys are in their rooms studying."

I mentally rolled my eyes at *that* idea. Neither Jake nor Julian, my younger brother, are what you'd call great students. They're generally happy if they get Cs, and my parents are completely ecstatic if they bring home a B. I'm definitely considered the "smart one" in the family; if I brought home a C my parents would freak out. I can usually live up to it, but once in awhile I think it might be nice to not have all that pressure.

No, I was willing to bet that Julian was in his room playing Nintendo. Jake, on the other hand, was probably on the Internet hanging out in some Spanish-language chatroom. But parents like to stay in la-la land about stuff like that.

"Josey," Mom said hesitantly, in a way that made me stop admiring her pajamas and take another look at her.

My friends think my mom's really pretty and I guess they're right. She has thick, wavy brown hair and big dark eyes, and she's really thin, so she usually wears simple, classic stuff like khaki pants and sweaters from Eddie Bauer. When she's working, of course, she has to wear her American Airlines navy-blue-and-white combo; my mom's been a ticket agent at O'Hare ever since we kids were all in school. Having a mom who works for a major airline is great, because it means our whole family can fly for free, if we're willing to fly standby. We've been to lots of fun places; Hawaii, Aruba, the Virgin Islands, Costa Rica, you name it. And, of course, we've been to Mexico quite a few times.

Anyway, what caught my attention tonight was that my mom had an unusual flush in her cheeks that actually kind of reminded me of Brandon Burke. What's more, I could see that her eyes were dancing in a way that I didn't remember ever seeing before. She definitely looked excited about something.

"What? What is it?" I asked with anticipation. It occurred to me to wonder whether my parents had impulsively decided to plan a family vacation for the upcoming Thanksgiving holiday. If not Thanksgiving, I hoped it wasn't during the Christmas break; I didn't want to miss the Holidazzle dance, even if Sarah, Britt, and I were going as each other's dates, as usual.

"Honey," my mom said, looking almost nervous. "I need to talk to you about something. Would you like something to drink, some cocoa maybe? I was going to pour a cup of coffee for myself."

Most people know better than to drink coffee at ten o'clock at night, but my parents never give it a second thought. They drink it from the moment they get out of bed in the morning; I can't remember a day of my life when I didn't awaken to the smell of coffee already brewing.

"No thanks," I said. "I'm still full from studying."

"Diet Coke and Doritos?" Mom asked, chuckling. She'd bought the supplies for many a study session in the past.

"Yeah, and M&Ms."

"Ugh. I don't know how you girls can concentrate with all those stimulants in your systems."

I raised an eyebrow and looked pointedly at the coffee cup she was filling, which made her laugh.

"I know, I know," she sighed. "And then there's the worst vice of all." She reached over to where her pack of Marlboro Light 100s lay on the table, pulling it toward her as she sank into a chair. "Just be glad *you* don't smoke."

Of course I had tried smoking before, but she didn't have to know that. My dad smokes too, but he's always trying to stop. Every couple of months he decides that he's coughing too much and vows to quit. He stomps around the house for a few days, chewing furiously on toothpicks and snapping at everyone, then decides maybe he's not ready to quit and goes back to smoking, much to everyone's relief. Mom never makes any pretense about wanting to quit. She says that smoking is like an old friend who's gotten her through some hard times.

"Come on, sit down," she said, pushing a kitchen chair toward me with her foot as she lit up. "I have something I want to tell you . . . big news, and I'm too excited to wait until tomorrow." She smiled at me. "I wanted to tell you before I told the boys."

She knew she had me then, of course. I sank into a chair and watched her take a drag and then expel the smoke in a smooth stream, waving it away absently with her hand in a gesture that's as familiar to me as the deep, warm sound of her laugh. She was smiling in a mysterious way, like she had a big secret.

I leaned forward to rub my eyes with the heels of my hands. They were tired from going over our notes in Sarah's bedroom, and the smoke from her cigarette was making them itch.

"Don't rub your eyes, you'll ruin your vision," Mom said reflexively, setting her cigarette down in the ashtray. I noticed that it was already overflowing with partially smoked butts; Mom must've broken her own record for cigarettes smoked in one evening.

"Well, what's the big news?" I asked. I really wasn't worried that the news was anything bad, since I doubted anything bad put that goofy look on her face.

Mom hesitated, reaching over absently to smooth a loose strand of hair behind one of my ears. She sat back and took another deep drag on her cigarette.

"Mom?" I unhooked my hair from behind my ear nervously. Now I *was* getting a little worried.

"Well, Josette, it's just that I have something to tell you, and it's something that's probably going to change your opinion of me forever . . . of both me *and* your father."

She took a deep breath, and set her half-smoked cigarette in the ashtray where it continued to smolder.

"There are some things that we've never discussed with you kids before, things that I'd always planned to tell you eventually, but up until now there didn't seem to be any reason to, and, well, now there *is*, and . . . oh, it's just such happy news!"

She broke off, grinning at me. I waited expectantly. I decided this definitely wasn't about a family trip.

Mom continued hesitantly, "Josey, I got a phone call tonight, a call from a social worker in North Dakota."

My mind tried to make sense of this information under the heading of "News That Would Make Mom Very Excited." Mom and Dad had both grown up in North Dakota. In fact, Grandma and Grandpa Muller, Dad's parents, still lived there, in Fargo, where we visited them a couple times a year.

"This social worker, her name was Cindy Richardson. She works for Lutheran Social Services in North Dakota, and she was calling on behalf of someone else. Someone who wants to get in touch with me." She stopped, nodding at me as if this was supposed to tell me more than it did.

After a moment's pause, I decided to help her out. "An old friend?" I offered. "Someone from high school?"

Mom swallowed and shook her head. She reached for her cigarette again, then changed her mind and left it in the ashtray where it sat.

I had an exciting thought. "Did someone die and leave you something? A bunch of money?" That would *certainly* be good news!

Mom shook her head, and tried to continue. "I feel it's important that I say this the right way, Josey, and I'm unsure of how to do that," she sighed. "I've been thinking all evening of how I was going to tell you about this and now here I am, talking in circles. I just want to be sure that you understand it all; what it means to your father and me, and to our family . . ."

Mom paused, still seeming to be at a loss for words. I'd never seen her like this before.

"Okay," she said finally, "I guess maybe I need to explain this in a roundabout way. Do you remember a few months ago, when I came home and caught Jake and Lilja up in his room and I kind of . . . overreacted?"

Did I *ever*. Jake and Lilja had been dating for almost a year and by now we were all used to seeing them curled up together on the family room couch, watching television. Just before school started, however, my mom had come home from work early one afternoon and found Jake and Lilja upstairs in Jake's room. I don't think they were actually having sex or anything, but Mom had a major meltdown about it. She ranted and raved about trust and maturity and appropriate behavior for a seventeen-year-old boy and his girlfriend, and blah, blah, blah. No one was surprised at first; Jake *had* crossed a major line, after all, but when several days had passed and she was still going on and on about it, we all started to wonder what was up with her. Being around mom during that week was like riding a rollercoaster; sometimes she'd be muttering to herself, and sometimes she'd be fuming, and other times she'd just sit there smoking and staring off into space. Twice, I saw her crying. In the end, Jake was actually begging for his punishment so that the whole mess could be over.

Dad didn't say much, just tiptoed around her like the rest of us, but he, too, seemed to be quieter than usual. Usually when Mom gets worked up about something he can talk her down. This time, though, no one seemed to know what to do.

So I said, *yeah*, I remembered, and didn't say much more about it. I didn't want to set her off again.

"I want you to understand what I couldn't tell you then, Josey. There was a reason that finding Jake and Lilja upstairs in Jake's room was so upsetting to me. It . . . it brought back memories of a very complicated and painful time in my life and with those memories came a lot of strong feelings. Some of which were probably evident to you."

And *how*.

"So," she said, her voice sounding steadier, "What I'm about to tell you will explain everything, and I really hope that you'll be just as thrilled about it as I am."

My mom drew in her breath as if she was about to dive into the deep end of the pool. She cast one last longing glance in the direction of her cigarettes, then turned to look me directly in the eye.

"Josey, the social worker was calling on behalf of a young woman named Audrey, who was looking for me. Audrey is, she's . . . part of our family."

I digested this calmly. A cousin maybe? I tried to think which side of the family she could be attached to. And why was Mom making such a big deal about a long-lost cousin?

Mom had reached over and put her cool hand on top of mine, "I know this is going to be hard for you to understand, but Audrey is . . . well, she's your sister. You've got an older sister, sweetie!"

2

I didn't say anything for a moment, as I let the words float around in my head, looking for a place to roost. A *sister?* How was that possible?

My mom was watching me nervously, waiting for my reaction.

"A sister?" was all I could repeat weakly.

"Yes, Josey," she nodded, her voice firmer now. "You have an older sister. Her name is Audrey . . . Audrey Merriday."

"But . . . where does she live? How come you never told me about this before?"

"Oh, honey," Mom sighed unhappily, finally giving in and reaching for her cigarette. "It was always such a painful thing for us. I don't think we really liked to think about it ourselves."

"What happened? Where is she?"

"Well, like I said, it's a long story. Dad and I were very young, just like Jake and Lilja. We made some mistakes and I got pregnant. We didn't even tell our parents or anyone. Dad had an aunt who lived down south and took in 'wayward girls,' and we hatched this foolish plan that when I got toward the end of the pregnancy, I'd go live with her until the baby was born. Then they'd have to let us get married. Or at least that's what we thought."

"How could no one tell that you were pregnant?"

Mom chuckled, remembering. "Well, I've always been thin, and the style of clothing at that time worked out perfectly; lots of smock tops and loose-fitting dresses. So I just sewed a few of my own things in home-ec class and I was right in style. No one suspected a thing."

She trailed off, her hand dropping absently to smooth the front of her flat stomach.

"And then when the baby came, you and Dad got married?"

Mom's smile faded as she stubbed out her cigarette and tapped a new one out of the pack. She took the first draw, then exhaled with a sigh.

"No, it didn't work out like we'd planned," she said. "When I was about eight months pregnant we wrote a letter to Dad's aunt, telling her that I was pregnant and needed to come and stay with her for awhile. We were so naïve. She immediately contacted Dad's parents."

"Grandpa and Grandma Muller?"

"Mm-hmm. She wrote them a letter," Mom shook her head, remembering. "A *letter*. I always thought that was so odd."

She looked at me. "Wouldn't you think a situation like that, your nephew announcing that he's secretly gotten his girlfriend pregnant, would have warranted an actual *phone call?*"

I raised my eyebrows, not knowing what to say. *A sister*, my mind whispered.

"Of course, when the letter arrived in Fargo all hell broke loose, as you might imagine. The next thing I knew, your father and I were sitting in Grandpa and Grandma Muller's living room along with my parents, and everyone was discussing how they were going to handle 'the situation.'"

"Were they mad?"

"Naturally. I don't remember much of what everyone said, except that it was the worst afternoon of my life. I *do* remember that there was lots of arguing about whose fault it was, and whose responsibility the baby was. My parents suggested that there were two options: Either we could get married or we could give the baby up for adoption. But your Dad's parents, Grandma and Grandpa Muller, wanted him to be able to go off to college without having to support a wife and baby. They were pretty determined that that was how things should be. And that really left only the one option."

Grandpa and Grandma Muller? It was hard to imagine

them being so cold and stubborn. What about the baby? Didn't they care about their own grandchild?

"But what did *you* want?"

Mom's look turned distant, and she reached over to stub her half-finished cigarette out bitterly. "Well, of course I wanted what I had always wanted; I wanted to have the baby, get married, and be a family."

She was silent for a moment, then shook her head. "Although to be fair, you must understand, Josette, how young and immature I was back then. I had absolutely no idea what getting married and raising a baby would mean at that age. After all, I was only sixteen; my head was full of all sorts of fairy-tale images. I guess the adults at the time knew better than I did. Or at least that's what they thought."

"But you and dad *did* get married," I pointed out in confusion.

"Yeah, but not until later." Mom suddenly looked tired, and for the first time I noticed that that her eyes were a little red around the rims, like she'd been crying.

"Anyway, my mom—your Grandma Charlotte—took me to an adoption agency in Fargo and made the arrangements. The whole thing seemed like a dream. A couple weeks later I went into labor and had the baby, a healthy little girl. I only saw her for a few seconds after she was born, they took her away so quickly. She cried for a moment, and I remember I wanted her to keep crying, so I could at least remember the way she sounded. But she quieted down, and then they took her off to the nursery. And that was it."

I was sad at the image of my mother at my age, lying helplessly on a hospital gurney as she watched her first-born child being carried away. "And you were all alone?"

"Oh, no, my mother was with me. She didn't have much to say, though, just sat by my bed."

She hesitated, a memory coming back to her. "Later, when she thought I was asleep, I overheard her on the phone. She must have been talking to Grandma Muller, and she sounded really angry. 'Are you going to have so many grandchildren that you can afford to give this one away?' she said. Grandma Muller must've thought she could, because the next thing I knew, I heard my mother slam down the phone."

Mom looked at me sadly. "It was years after that before they spoke to each other again," she added. "And even after they did, it's always been the elephant in the room that no one could mention."

I scanned back over my memories and realized that, indeed, my two sets of grandparents rarely visited at the same time, didn't often attend the same birthday celebrations, and almost never spent Christmas with us on the same year. Since they lived in different states, it had never occurred to me that maybe they were avoiding each other.

"But how could they not have spoken to each other at your wedding?" I asked, perplexed.

Mom snorted. "We got married by a justice of the peace the day I turned eighteen. None of our parents were at the ceremony; we didn't even tell them until afterwards."

My mind was reeling, trying to take it all in. A question suddenly occurred to me. "So what happened to the baby after that?"

"I never knew." My mom shook her head. "All these years I never let myself think about it if I could help it. After your father and I were married, we were living in married housing while your dad went to pharmacy school, and there was another family living there who had some adopted children. And they didn't treat those children very well. I don't even know whether the fact that they were adopted even had anything to do with it, but it was so painful for me. I felt it was a sure sign that wherever my baby was, she was not being treated well, and I felt horribly responsible for that. My child was living a terrible life because of my own mistakes. The only way I could live with the guilt was to push everything out of my mind as much as I could and try to move on."

She looked so sad as she finished that I wanted to find some way to reassure her. "You did the best you could, Mom," I said earnestly, leaning forward. "You had no choice."

Mom looked up at me. "Well, I appreciate that, Josey," she replied. "That's very generous. And I guess you're probably right; at the time it truly *did* seem like there were no other options available to me. It's just hard looking back as an adult and seeing that perhaps there *were*.

"And that, in a nutshell, is why it was so upsetting to me to find Jake and Lilja in Jake's bedroom together. It's not so much that they were doing anything wrong. It's just that I saw so much *potential* for wrongness, for mistakes that no one could take back and that would possibly have an impact on their lives, and the lives of others, forever."

I nodded, understanding now. "And it made you remember."

"And it made me remember."

We sat quietly for a moment. There was so much to digest. Mom was right; hearing what she had to tell me had changed my understanding of who my mother was, of what painful secrets she carried in her heart. My head was full and there was an unfamiliar heavy feeling in my chest. The television was still playing in the family room, and the canned laughter seemed out of place as the background to our conversation.

"What does Daddy think about all of this?"

"Your father has had his pain about it too, I'm sure. Like I said, we don't talk about it."

I tried to imagine my father as a young man of sixteen, sitting helplessly in his parents' living room while his future was decided. He was so protective of my mom now that it was hard to picture him not arguing with his parents or proposing that he and my mom run away together under the cover of darkness, like they do in romance novels.

"Josey," Mom said, interrupting my thoughts. "I'm sure that what I've told you here has changed your perspective about a lot of things, and I hope that you won't judge us too harshly. We didn't mean to hurt anyone, and we would never again allow one of our own children to be taken from us in that way. I've had to forgive a lot of people for the events of that time, including myself, and I hope you can find it in your heart to forgive me, and your father, as well."

She reached out and picked up both my hands from where they had been lying on top of the table, pressing them between hers.

"But tonight," she said, her eyes regaining the shine they had earlier, "tonight something wonderful has happened that may give us a happy ending after all these years of sorrow."

I had almost forgotten that this conversation had started out with my mom smiling in that strange, sparkly way. "About the . . . baby." I'd meant to say "sister," but the word had gotten stuck somewhere between my brain and my mouth.

"Yes," my mom shook her head, "Only the 'baby' is a grown woman now. She's twenty-five years old! You have a twenty-five-year-old sister, can you imagine? And the social worker called because Audrey has contacted the agency that handled the adoption; she wants to have contact with us, Josey! Only the agency had to get our permission before they could give her any information about us."

"And did you give it?"

Mom gave me a surprised look. "Of course I did!"

I smiled as I nodded *of course* back to her, but my face felt stiff and strange.

A worried look suddenly clouded Mom's face. "My concern, though, is that Audrey probably has no idea that her father and I ever married, much less that we went on to have three more children. That's going to come as a tremendous shock to her. I can't imagine."

She considered this seriously for a moment, then broke into a smile.

"I almost forgot to mention the best part of all, Josey. The best part is that Cindy said Audrey's had a good life, a *wonderful* life with loving parents, not the terrible life my own guilt made me imagine. I'm just so happy and relieved; I don't even know how to put it into words!"

Mom's eyes filled with tears, and she pulled her hands from mine to wipe them away. Her head bent forward, and suddenly her shoulders were heaving with sobs. I jumped up from my chair to wrap my arms around her in an awkward hug.

"It's okay, Mom," I soothed. "In fact, it's great. I have a sister, an older sister that I never thought I'd have! I can't believe it!"

I really couldn't. My whole life I'd thought of my parents as being completely perfect people as far as parents go, and now I'd learned that they were far from it. And my whole life I'd been the only girl in the family, a sister with two brothers, and now suddenly that was no longer true either. I had a sister, almost ten years older than I was. It was all going to be an adjustment, sure, but I really believed it when I said it: "I'm so happy, Mom! It's *great* news!"

3

The next morning I overslept, which left me with little time to do anything besides scramble to shower, dress, and grab a cold cherry Pop-Tart before I took off running for the bus stop. Jake's supposed to give me a ride to school, but he leaves me if I'm running late, so, frankly, I'm pretty used to riding the bus. When it comes to punctuality, Jake's and my personalities are completely opposite of what you'd expect; he's always on time and I'm always late. His leaving me behind is a frequent source of conflict between us, but I can't really argue when my parents point out that Jake shouldn't have to pay the price for my dawdling.

This morning I actually didn't mind riding the bus, since doing so gave me time to sit back and consider everything my mom had told me at our kitchen table the night before. I still couldn't believe that I had an older sister; it seemed like the whole shape of our family had changed with those words. My mom didn't have much of the important information yet, like what Audrey looked like or what kind of person she was, so it was still hard for me to really imagine her. We knew only that she lived in Grand Forks, about an hour north of my grandparents' home in Fargo, and that she had wanted to make contact with her "birth mother." My mom.

I wondered for a moment what Audrey's reaction would be upon discovering that the two people who had made her had also given birth to three other children: me, Jake, and Julian. In a way, it made me feel sorry for her, because I imagined it would feel pretty weird to discover that you'd grown up as a part of an entirely different family, while your *real* family was off somewhere else. The social worker herself had been surprised when Mom told her that she and Dad had gotten married and had more children; she told Mom that it was very unusual to encounter a situation like this. *She's not kidding*, I thought. *I'd certainly never have imagined it myself.*

The plan now, according to my mom, was for the social worker to call Audrey back with the news that she had spoken with my mom, tell her about the situation, and let her know that my parents were agreeable to having contact.

"Can you imagine that Cindy was calling to get our *permission* for Audrey to make contact with us? To give our names to her?" my mom had said in disbelief. "As if we'd ever refuse her that!"

"Well, maybe there are some people who don't want to be found," I considered out loud.

"I can't imagine!" My mom shook her head. "That would be like denying Audrey the right to her identity!"

The bus pulled up in front of the school and the door opened with a *whoosh*, sending cold October air rushing down the aisle toward me. I stayed in my seat, letting the other students get off ahead of me. It had taken me a long time to fall asleep after I went to bed last night, and I was feeling kind of tired.

"Hey, you're late!" Britt said, when she saw me coming down the hall toward my locker.

"Someone got stuck taking the bus again," commented Sarah with a wry smile. Britt, Sarah, and I always convened at my locker in the mornings so we could walk to class together. Sarah and I had Algebra II, while Britt was repeating Algebra I.

I rolled my eyes and made a sour face; I didn't have the energy to think up a witty comeback. Fortunately, it didn't matter.

"Guess who we saw outside of the Life Skills Room!" bubbled Britt, her brown eyes glowing with excitement.

"I can't guess."

"Brandon Burke! And he was eating a banana!" she squealed.

Sarah and I exchanged a look. Sometimes it almost seemed as if we were the parents and Britt was our giddy child.

"An actual banana?" I teased her. "Ordinary *fruit?* I didn't think demigods ate real food like the rest of us lowly beings."

Britt looked confused. "What's a demi-gob?" she asked, but her question was drowned out by the bell that signaled the warning for first period. The current of bodies around us began to move more purposefully toward their various destinations. I hurriedly threw my jacket and extra books into my locker and we joined the throng heading to classes. It looked like I'd have to wait until later to share my news with Sarah and Britt.

The morning passed uneventfully, aside from the psychology test third hour, which went well. Even Britt seemed optimistic as we met for lunch in the cafeteria.

"I'm sure glad we spent so much time on the id, ego, and superego last night," she said. "There were actually questions about that stuff!"

"Yeah, I hate it when you kill yourself studying things that they never even ask about," Sarah agreed, nodding. She looked around. "Where shall we plant ourselves, ladies?"

We surveyed the available seats, looking for three together. Early in the fall most kids brought their lunch and ate it outside, but now that the weather was getting colder the lunchroom was becoming crowded.

"Over there!" I said, pointing with my elbow. We had nearly made it across the room when out of nowhere a hard roll thudded onto on Sarah's tray.

"Good grief," she growled, glaring over in the general

direction from which the missile had originated. Looking around, I spied a table of boys who seemed a little *too* interested in their lunch trays. We all knew that the likely launcher was Josh Marto, and our suspicions were confirmed by the fact that the boys who weren't smirking at their lunch trays were smirking at *him*. Josh had been teasing Sarah since he moved to Woodridge in the eighth grade, and although she claimed she thought he was a complete dork, it was pretty obvious by the high color in her cheeks that that wasn't the *whole* truth.

"Ugh, the boys in our class are so *juvenile*," Sarah said fiercely, setting her tray on the table with a clatter for emphasis. Britt's only response was to begin munching on a carrot stick, and I really had nothing to add either.

"So, what else is new?" Britt asked a few minutes later, peeling the lid from her container of raspberry yogurt. Apparently BB eating a banana didn't warrant rehashing.

"Well," I mentioned casually. "My mom dropped an A-bomb on me last night when I got home."

"Why?" asked Britt, licking yogurt off the lid. "You weren't late."

"No, it was something else. She told me . . . well, apparently I have an older sister I never knew about."

I didn't look up as I said it, as if spreading ranch dressing evenly over my salad required all of my concentration at the moment. When I looked up, both of my friends were staring at me; Britt's first spoonful of yogurt was hovering halfway between the cup and her mouth, and Sarah's eyebrows were raised so high they had disappeared under her bangs entirely.

"A sister?" Britt finally said. "What are you talking about?"

I tried to affect a nonchalant tone. "Well, last night when I got home, my mom told me that she and my dad had a baby when they were in high school, and their parents made them give it up for adoption. And now she . . . the baby . . . decided to look us up."

I speared a forkful of salad but didn't have the energy to bring it to my mouth. My stomach was suddenly feeling a little woozy anyway.

Britt's mouth was hanging open, but she quickly recovered.

"You are *kidding* me! How old is she? What's her name? Where does she live? Does she look like you? Are you going to—"

"Whoa!" Sarah held up a hand, interrupting Britt's barrage of questions. She peered at me across the table, a serious look on her face. "But Josey, weren't you shocked? What did you think when your mom told you that you have a sister that you never knew about?"

I smiled gratefully at her concern. Sarah could always be trusted to get right to the heart of things.

"I don't know, really," I admitted. "I'm happy, I guess. I haven't had much time to get used to the idea. My mom just kind of hit me with everything when I got home last night. I don't even think she'd planned to tell me about it until I was older, but a social worker had called from North Dakota to say that she—her name is Audrey—was searching for her birth mother. Which is my mom."

"Doesn't she want to find your dad too?"

"She doesn't *know* that my parents got married and had more kids. Or maybe she does by now. I don't know; the social worker was going to call her back and tell her the whole thing, I guess."

Sarah said nothing for a minute. Even Britt was uncharacteristically quiet, alternating between staring at me and her lunch.

"Come on, you guys, eat," I urged them, gesturing toward their trays. "We've only got fifteen minutes left."

Sarah shrugged and pushed her plate away. "I'm not really hungry anyway," she said as Britt went back to her yogurt. "What else do you know about her?" she asked.

"Well, let's see. She still lives in North Dakota . . . that's where my parents grew up . . . and she's twenty-five."

"Twenty-five?"

"Yeah." At our age, twenty-five seemed like a different generation entirely.

"That's ten years older than us," commented Britt through a mouthful of yogurt.

"Than *we*," Sarah and I both automatically corrected her.

We were silent for a minute, Britt finished her yogurt, while I picked at my salad and Sarah ignored her slice of pizza. Around us, the usual lunchroom chaos swirled as other students yelled back and forth to each other, tossed the occasional food item, and generally ate lunch.

"So what's going to happen now?" Sarah asked finally. "With your . . . sister, I mean."

"I don't know," I admitted. "I guess she'll write us or call us herself. Or maybe she'll come to visit."

The last idea was a bit unnerving; it was one thing to know that Audrey was out there somewhere and quite another to imagine her in my own house.

"Wow, wouldn't that be great?" exclaimed Britt. "I wonder if she looks like you!"

I wondered that too. I was trying to imagine what it would be like to have an older sister for the rest of my life, one that to my knowledge had never even existed before last night.

"On the other hand, she might be completely different from you," Sarah proposed, looking nervous. "What if she's stuck up or obnoxious?"

"Yeah, or maybe she's mean, like a wicked stepsister," Britt snickered.

Sarah shot her an impatient look. "No, but seriously, Josey, what if she's *angry* or something? I mean, here she is growing up in North Dakota and the rest of her family, her parents and brothers and sister, are all the way over here in Illinois. It's like she was *the missing face on your Christmas card* or something."

I didn't know what to say to that. I had never considered that Audrey might be upset about finding out that she had an entire family in Illinois who had not bothered to look for her.

"I'm just saying," Sarah went on earnestly, "that these reunions with adopted kids don't always go smoothly. I saw that happen once on *The Maury Povich Show*. It started out with a happy reunion, and the next thing you know, everybody's trying to choke each other."

"Well, I *hope* it doesn't happen like that," I said uncertainly. "I'm sure the social worker would have warned us if she was unbalanced or something."

"They don't always seem like they're crazy right away," Sarah said seriously. "It takes time before everyone figures it out."

Unfortunately, at that moment the bell sounded for fifth period, and we had to fight our way to the garbage cans to clear off our trays. Sarah's comments had given me things to think about, though. I was no longer sure that having a new big sister was guaranteed to be a good experience.

Nevertheless, when I ran into Jake between fifth and sixth period I couldn't help but take advantage of the situation. Maybe I was still a little annoyed with him for leaving me to ride the bus that morning, or maybe I was feeling upset about what Sarah had said, but I decided to drop the news on him as abruptly as Mom had dropped it on me the night before.

"So, how was the bus this morning?" Jake greeted me with a smirk as I fell into step beside him. "Was the floor as sticky as usual?"

I knew I only had a few minutes before we arrived at Jake's English class and I'd be walking on without him.

"Um, did you see Mom this morning before she left?" I asked casually, hurrying to keep up.

"Nope." He shook his head. "She was gone before I got out of the shower."

"Hmm, then I guess she didn't get a chance to tell you." I shrugged indifferently.

"Tell me what?"

I paused, relishing the moment. Not too long, though, because we were already coming up outside of Jake's class. I slowed my pace.

"It's just that Mom told me something *really* big last night when I got home from Sarah's," I said, stopping with him to adjust my books. "You won't believe it."

"Uh, listen, maybe you'd better fill me in later," Jake said, glancing nervously into his classroom. "We're probably going to have a quiz and I haven't even looked my notebook over yet."

I ignored him; I wasn't about to miss the opportunity to be the one to break the news. "Mom and Dad had another kid . . . before us," I blurted. "Her name is Audrey and she lives in North Dakota. You know, near where Grandma and Grandpa Muller live."

It seemed as if Jake hadn't heard me at first. Then he looked at me hard, squinting, as if he couldn't see me clearly.

"What?"

"I'm not kidding," I said, studying my fingernails as if

they interested me more than he did. I was enjoying this. "They had another kid; a girl. She's ten years older than I am; that means she's eight years older than you are."

The halls were clearing out but suddenly Jake didn't seem in as much of a hurry to get into his classroom.

"What?" he said again. His face had gone pale, and I suddenly wondered whether it had been such a good idea for me to tell him after all.

"Uh, your class is starting," I reminded him gently. "You'd probably better go in."

He automatically turned to go in, then hesitated and turned back toward me. "Are you messing with me?" he demanded.

I shook my head.

"Really. Wow, that's so weird. I can't believe it," he said. Before I could respond, he disappeared into his classroom.

As I hurried down the hall toward my own class, making it inside just before the bell rang, it occurred to me that Jake probably wasn't going to do very well on his English quiz. It was funny, I thought; we hadn't even met Audrey and she was already making such a big impact on our lives. Little did I know that it was only the beginning.

4

When I walked in the door after school I was nearly bowled over by Julian, who accosted me before I even had my coat off.

"J-J-Jake said that you told him there's another k-k-kid in our family," he stammered. Julian stuttered a lot when he was younger, but now that he's twelve he only does it when he's really nervous or excited about something. Hearing it always makes me feel protective of him, like I want to hug him.

"Yeah," I agreed. "Mom told me about it last night." I quickly filled him in on the details of what I knew.

"That's so cool," he said. "Does Dad know?"

I made a face. "Of course he does, you idiot. It's not the kind of thing that Mom would keep to herself."

"D-do you think she'll come here?" He looked a little anxious. "To live, I mean?"

I chuckled. "No, silly. I suppose she might come to visit, but I doubt she'd move here. She's a grown-up, after all. She probably has her own house. Or maybe she lives in an apartment. Anyway, I doubt she's going to want to move in."

Julian considered this. "Does she have any kids? Maybe I'm an uncle and you're an aunt."

"I don't know," I admitted. "I suppose she might." It was occurring to me that there were many things about Audrey that we didn't know yet. I wondered when we'd find out. Would the social worker call us back after she talked to Audrey? Or were we supposed to call her? Scariest of all, would she call us *here*, at our house? The idea made my stomach flip over. Just then the phone rang, making me jump a foot.

"Hello?" Julian was already answering it before I could recover.

"Just a minute," I heard him say, and he handed the phone to me.

I took it nervously, but it was only Sarah. "Listen," she said. "I just wanted to tell you that I was sorry about what I said in the lunchroom today. About your sister, and her possibly being a psycho."

"Oh . . . don't worry about it."

She was quiet for a minute, and I could hear her breathing on the other end. "What do you really think she'll be like?" she asked finally.

"I don't know. Probably something like my mom. She's a lot older than we are, after all."

"But she's closer to our age than to your mom's," Sarah pointed out. "I think she'll be a lot like you."

"Anyway," she continued, "this'll be a real test of the 'nature versus nurture' thing, like we studied back in Intro to Psychology last year."

"True." I hadn't thought of that, and now it gave me an idea. We had to write an independent research paper for Mrs. Gasparini's class; maybe I could use this! I made a mental note to jot down a few things as soon as I got off the phone.

"If you think about it," Sarah said, warming to the subject, "it's kind of like that girl who was abandoned as a baby and was raised by wolves . . ."

Good grief. "Well, I don't think she was raised by *wolves*, exactly," I told her. "Mom said her adoptive parents were both teachers."

"Oh." She sounded slightly disappointed. "Well, anyway, you have to admit it's still pretty interesting. Because technically, she has the same genetics as you have, but grew up in an entirely separate environment."

I chuckled. "For a future lawyer, you're thinking an awful lot like a psychologist."

"Yeah, well, lawyers have to understand things about human nature too." Sarah considered the situation. "So you're not even a tiny bit nervous?" she asked finally.

"No. Not really." But I knew I was lying, and probably she did too.

I heard Sarah's mom calling for her.

"Just a minute," she said to me. She covered the phone and I could hear her holler something back. There was a brief, muffled exchange before she came back on.

"So, what are you doing now?"

"I don't know, homework, I suppose. And it's my week to put the laundry away."

"Yuck, I hate putting laundry away. I'm on dishes this week."

"I hate dishes worse than laundry. I'm too young to have dishpan hands."

"That's what I tell my mom, but she just tells me that it's better to have wrinkled hands full of allowance money than smooth ones that are empty."

"She makes a point."

"Yep. Hey, I bumped right into Brandon Burke outside of the counselor's office this afternoon! I just about died!" She laughed. "I was so close to him I could see a little scab on his cheek, right by his ear. Do you suppose he cut himself shaving or something?"

"Do you think he shaves? He doesn't even look like he has any whiskers." We reflected on this for a moment.

"What was he wearing?"

"His Bears jersey."

"Ooh, I love him in that."

"Me too. And you know what?"

"What?

"I could smell his cologne. I think it was *CK for Men*."

I sighed. "Did you actually touch him?"

"We kind of bumped shoulders," Sarah said. "Oh, and I just remembered something: He said, 'Sorry.'"

"You actually *talked* to him?!"

"Well, to the extent that he said the one word to me, yes."

"Still, he said it right *to* you." None of us had actually exchanged words with BB before. This was a groundbreaking development indeed.

"I think this means you guys are dating," I pointed out.

Sarah laughed. "Hopefully."

We spent a few more minutes recalling prior BB sightings. Sarah made me promise to let her be the one to tell Britt the details of her collision with Brandon Burke, and we hung up.

After I got off the phone I ate a bowl of my favorite cereal, Lucky Charms, before dragging my backpack up to my room to start my homework. I changed into my Russells for comfort and was deep into my algebra assignment when my dad poked his head in the door.

"Hi, Dad," I said. "I didn't know that you were home."

"How was your day, Josey Posey?" He leaned against the doorframe, and I noticed he was wearing the grey V-neck sweater I love. It makes him look kind of young and sporty.

"Fine. The usual." I doubted he'd be interested in hearing about Sarah's encounter with Brandon Burke.

"Good, good . . ." He paused, then cleared his throat, and looked as if he wanted to say something more. I realized suddenly that he wanted to bring up the Audrey thing.

"So, pretty weird about this other kid, huh?" I said helpfully, to get him started.

He smiled and looked relieved. "Yeah, I suppose it *is* weird, in a way."

"It's cool though."

"Isn't it?" Dad looked at me hopefully. "I'm glad you feel that way, Josey."

He shifted, looking a little uneasy. "You know, it all happened when your mother and I were so young. We really didn't know what we were doing. Well, we knew what we were *doing* . . ." he trailed off awkwardly, and seemed to be searching for the right words.

Finally he said, "I just don't want you to think that we had this child and gave her away and then we never thought about her again. It's been a very painful hole in our hearts all these years."

"Kind of like the missing face on our Christmas card," I supplied helpfully, borrowing Sarah's lunchroom comment.

He looked at me oddly. "Yeah . . . kind of like that."

"Don't worry, Dad, I don't think it's a bad thing. In fact I think it's great," I said enthusiastically. "I mean, I finally have a sister. Even if she *is* a lot older than I am."

Dad came over to where I was sitting to give me a hug. "Thanks for understanding, sweetie. I guess I need you to understand that people can make mistakes when they're young and naïve that they regret for the rest of their lives. And now maybe we have a chance to make this one right."

I smiled at him, and he smiled back at me. He was close enough that I could see the friendly little crinkles around his eyes that I don't usually notice. Dad's still pretty handsome and young-looking, for a dad anyway. It was going to be hilarious if it turned out that he was already someone's grandpa.

I finished my homework just before my dad called us down for dinner. Since my mom works until at least seven every night and then has to commute home, my dad makes most of the meals in our house. Not that I'm complaining, because he's a great cook. Tonight we were having chicken, couscous, and asparagus. Julian chattered away like he usually does, but I noticed that Jake seemed unusually quiet, picking at the food he normally wolfs down. I even tried to pick a fight with him over who had to clean up after dinner but he wouldn't fight back, so I just gave up and did it myself.

Afterwards, I was walking past his room when I saw him lying on his bed, staring at the television.

"Hey," I said, pausing in the doorway. "Um, look; I'm sorry if I kind of shocked you today at school. I shouldn't have hit you with all that stuff in the hall like I did."

He shrugged, not taking his eyes off of the screen. "It's okay," he said. "I was just surprised."

"Yeah, I was surprised when Mom told me, too. Did Dad say anything to you about it?"

"Yeah, he gave me the whole 'we were too young, just like you and Lilja' speech."

I laughed. "Mom said this is why she freaked out when she caught you guys upstairs that time."

He rolled his eyes. "I figured that one out already."

"Well, anyway; isn't it weird?"

"Nah, I'm already kind of getting used to the idea."

"Yeah, me too." It was funny how quickly I was adjusting my concept of "our family" to include this faceless person named Audrey. That reminded me that I wanted to make some notes for my "nature versus nurture" project, so I went on to my room and got out my notebook. I wrote down the few things that I already knew about Audrey, and then began to record similar information about myself.

Born: Woodridge, Illinois, I wrote. *Birthdate: September 26.*

I thought about what else I should include. I suppose it could be anything, really. I jotted down some possible category ideas: personality, likes and dislikes, and hobbies. I thought about the first category; it was hard to think of how to describe my own personality. I wrote down: *Smart*, then crossed it off a minute later, thinking that it sounded too much like bragging. It didn't really fit under the heading of "personality" anyway. Maybe it would be easier to get a more objective idea of my personality traits by asking Sarah and Britt.

Under "Hobbies" I wrote: *Hanging out with friends, reading, traveling, shopping, going to the movies.*

I thought a minute, and then began to come up with other categories.

Favorite color: orange
Favorite kind of food: Mexican
Favorite movie: "I Know What You Did Last Summer"
Favorite book: Harriet the Spy
Favorite clothes: Abercrombie, Gap, Old Navy
Favorite perfume: Dream (by Gap)
Most admired person: Sigmund Freud
Favorite sport: *cross-country running* (of course)

Under *Dislikes* I wrote: *People who are fake, or who lie.* After another moment I added *cauliflower.*

I couldn't really think of anything else, so I closed my notebook and slid it into my backpack. It was time for bed anyway. I was digging through my dresser drawer searching for my favorite blue pajamas with the little moons on them when I remembered that I hadn't put the laundry away.

A quick check of the laundry room revealed that there were indeed several folded baskets waiting. I groaned to myself. Jake and Julian could put their own stuff away this week, I decided. Just as I was bringing up the last load Mom came in the door from the garage. She looked beat.

"Long day?" I asked her sympathetically.

"Yeah, and a long drive home." She gave me a tired hug. "How about you? How was your day?"

"Fine. Nothing special."

Mom sighed, and I could hear how exhausted she was. "Are you still feeling okay?" she asked. "About everything from last night, I mean?"

"Yes, I'm cool with it, Mom." To tell you the truth, I'd thought about Audrey enough for one day. I was getting tired of the subject.

"Good. I sure hope that we hear from her soon."

"Is she going to call us?"

Mom frowned. "Actually, I don't know. The social worker just said that she'd be getting back to Audrey, and then the ball would be in her court."

I considered this. "What if she doesn't contact us?"

Mom's forehead wrinkled. "I can't imagine that she wouldn't, after having gone to the trouble of tracking us down. Although it *did* occur to me that she might be overwhelmed to find out that she's ended up with five new people rather than just the one she was hoping to find. Who knows; maybe she'll need some time to adjust to the whole thing."

Mom's eyes suddenly grew moist. "To tell you the truth, I really have no idea how she'll react, Josey. I don't even know . . . what kind of person she is."

I shifted the heavy basket of laundry resting awkwardly on my hip. "Mom, I'm sure she'll be fine with it. Don't worry."

"I hope you're right." Mom dabbed at her eyes with the sleeve of her coat, which she was still wearing. "Oh Josey," she sighed again. "This whole thing is so draining. It's all I could think about all day."

I pictured my mom at work, printing out boarding passes and making seat assignments, her head filled all the while with thoughts of Audrey. An unexpected bubble of jealousy rose up in my chest and lodged in my throat, where it stuck uncomfortably. Part of me felt a little glad that Mom was finding Audrey's sudden appearance in our lives "draining."

"Yeah, I'll bet it's a big shock for you and Dad."

"To tell you the truth, I'm not *totally* shocked," she responded. "I figured someday we might hear from her. If she's anything like I was at her age, she's on a quest to understand herself better. I wouldn't be able to just go through life without knowing the full story of who I was, would you? She must be kind of curious. You know . . . a thinker."

Like *me*, I thought.

Mom noticed the laundry basket. "Sweetie, it's late; you should be in bed. Why don't you let me finish up with those?"

"Okay," I let her take the basket and leaned over to accept her goodnight kiss. "'Night, Mom."

"'Night, Josey."

I brushed my teeth and puttered around my room for awhile, waiting for the heavy feeling over my heart to dissipate, but it was still there as I crawled under the covers.

After lying there for a few moments, I got out of bed and pulled my "nature versus nurture" notebook out of my backpack. On the page about Audrey I made a new heading. *Personality*, I wrote, and underneath it: *Curious*.

Maybe my mom was right, maybe Audrey *would* need some time to think about things once she found out that a whole family awaited her in Woodridge, rather than just the one person she had been seeking. And maybe that wouldn't be such a bad thing. It would give us *all* time to think about things.

5

Two days later I had my own Brandon Burke encounter to report. I was coming out of Algebra when I looked up and spotted BB leaning against the opposite wall, near the drinking fountain. He had his book bag slung over one shoulder, and he wasn't alone; Charlie Goodall and Cody Raasch, two other members of the cross-country team, were with him.

Just as the realization was setting in that *I* was having an actual up-close-and-personal BB sighting, he glanced up and our eyes met. Unfortunately, the unnatural feeling of Brandon's cool blue eyes locked onto mine affected me like a deer in the headlights, and I stopped in my tracks, helpless to move. A split second later I was freed from my paralysis, however, by a rough shove from behind.

"What's yer problem?!" demanded Travis Hansen. Travis was a fullback on the Woodridge High football team and generally shouldered his way through the hallways as if the rest of us were all members of the opposing team. The force that was Travis knocked me forward, smack into the unyielding chest of Brandon Burke.

I had a moment to confirm that BB was, indeed, wearing *CK for Men* before I recoiled in horror, springing backward to land squarely on my behind in the middle of the hall.

"Hey, watch it, dude! You knocked her down!"

Even in my horribly disadvantaged state, I managed to sneak a look at my defender, and was surprised to see that Charlie Goodall, his face red, was glaring accusingly up at Travis the Tank.

Travis halted momentarily in his momentum to regard Charlie, obviously deciding whether or not it was worth the time and effort to remind Charlie who he was talking to. Apparently he decided it was not.

"Yeah? Well, *bite* me," he snarled, before he resumed barreling down the hall. "Tell her to get her skinny butt out of the way." Only he didn't say "butt."

Now Charlie, Brandon, and Cody were all looking right at me. Charlie reached down to help me up, but I scrambled to my feet, flapping my hands like an idiot to shoo him away. "It's fine! I'm okay! Thanks!" I shrilled, jockeying my books back into position.

"Are you really okay?" Charlie asked, his expression

concerned. I'd never realized before what dark brown eyes he had.

"Yup, no problem!" I chirped. "Well, gotta get to class!" I darted off down the hall in the direction that Travis had gone, my head swimming. As I turned the corner I heard a raucous burst of laughter and look back, horrified that Brandon Burke and his friends were now laughing about what a dork I was. It was a different group of kids, however, and they weren't even looking at me. Charlie, Cody, and BB were gone.

I recounted the whole painful episode to Britt and Sarah over lunch.

"Thank God it wasn't *me*," breathed Britt.

Sarah was equally sympathetic. "At least now I don't feel so bad about barging into him on Monday," she chuckled.

"Hmm, well, thank you *both* for your support," I sniffed.

"Actually, I'm kind of jealous of you two," Britt pouted. She took a bite of her sandwich.

"Jealous?!" Sarah and I exclaimed together, incredulous.

Britt finished chewing and swallowed her mouthful. "I'm serious! At least you both got to have direct contact with BB; I haven't even seen him for weeks!"

"Maybe you could throw yourself in front of his car after school today," suggested Sarah dryly.

Britt made a face at her. She considered, "I wonder if

I should drop chemistry to get into his third period study hall."

"What? And abandon your dream of becoming a rocket scientist?" I snorted, regretting the words as soon as they were out of my mouth. Britt's face fell and Sarah shot me a look.

"Oh, Britt, I didn't mean anything by—" I tried, but it was too late.

"I guess I'm done eating," Britt snapped, jumping up abruptly and grabbing her tray. Sarah and I watched her flounce away, her red ponytail swinging.

"Gee, where'd that crack come from?" Sarah asked, "You know how sensitive she is about us thinking she's not as smart as we are."

"I know. I don't know why I said it. I guess I'm just kind of crabby today."

"Still . . . she's probably in the bathroom crying right now."

"Yeah," I nodded. "I'd better go track her down and apologize."

I found her in the second floor bathroom. Her Skechers were visible under one of the stalls, and I could hear her sniffling.

"Britt," I said, genuinely sorry. "Look, I don't know why I even said something so mean. I'm a complete jerk."

"Just because I don't get all As like you and Sarah doesn't mean I'm dumb, you know," she hiccupped indignantly from behind the wall.

"I know."

The stall door swung open and Britt emerged. Her nose was red and her eyes were watery; I felt worse just seeing them.

"I know it's not an excuse, but I'm just in a really bad mood today. It was so embarrassing to fall on my butt in front of Brandon and his friends. I looked like such a moron."

She washed her hands, ignoring me. "Mr. Lynn said that if I can pass Algebra this time and keep my GPA up, I should have no problem getting accepted at the Tech."

"I'm sure you'll get in. And you'll make a great medical technologist or whatever it is."

"Phlebotomy technician. They draw blood."

"Oh, yeah."

"Lots of people are squeamish about blood, you know. But not me."

"Not I." The correction came out of my mouth before I could catch it. We stared at each other for a moment, as Britt's expression hardened.

"Whatever!" she snapped before I could apologize again, and stormed past me and out of the bathroom.

I regarded myself in the mirror over the sink. What was the term my mom had used to describe things right now? Oh yeah, *draining*. That about summed it up.

The rest of the school day passed in a haze. I could hardly wait to get home and take a nap; maybe I was coming down with something.

A nap wasn't in my future, however. Julian was again waiting for me at the door.

"She sent a letter!" he shouted, even though I was only a foot away from him. "Already! Look!" He held out a slim white business envelope, slightly rumpled from his sweaty boy-grasp. I took it from him with my fingertips and sat down in the big chair in the family room.

"Geez, Julian, you've almost messed it up."

He ignored me and bent over my shoulder as we both studied the sealed envelope. It told no tales of what was inside; even the stamp had a nondescript American flag motif.

"Should we open it?" Julian suggested hopefully.

I shook my head with regret. "Mmm, I don't think we'd better. Look, it's addressed to Mom, not to us."

I studied the handwritten address. The letters were small and round, but I noticed that Audrey made her capital As the same way I did; a flowy, printed *A* rather than the proper, rounded cursive ones we'd been taught in school. I wondered whether handwriting was determined by genetics or learning.

Audrey Merriday, 3300 Lincoln Drive, Grand Forks, ND.
My sister.

It would no longer be *"Jake, Josey, and Julian"*; from here on out my parents would refer to their children as *"Jake, Josey, Julian, and Audrey."* Or would Audrey's name come first, since she was the oldest?

"Let's call Mom; maybe she'll tell us to open it," Julian proposed. He was already dialing.

"Anne Muller, please," I heard him say in his polite phone voice. I was surprised he wasn't stuttering today, as excited as he was. I went upstairs to change clothes, and when I came down he was just hanging up.

"She says we can open it if we're careful and don't tear it or anything," he reported, his face eager.

I frowned, feeling kind of insulted. "Like we're going to *tear* it."

Julian was already starting to pry open the envelope. "Give me that!" I tried to snatch it away from him. "You'll ruin it."

He held it out of my reach, looking wounded. "I'll be careful."

"Just let me open it, and then we'll both read it."

"Okay, but if there are any pictures I get to look at them first."

"Hmmm . . ."

"Promise!"

"Al*right.*"

Reluctantly, he handed the letter over to me. I went over to the roll-top desk and dug around until I found the letter opener that Mom uses when she pays bills. We both watched as I slid the opener underneath the flap of the envelope and lifted it up, slicing neatly through the creased edge. Julian peered inside.

"Ha, there is a picture!" he crowed. "I get it, remember?" There was no choice but to pluck it from the envelope with my fingertips and hand it over to him, face down.

"Should we read the letter first or look at the picture?"

"Picture," he decided, already turning it over to look. I held my breath. "Well?"

Julian grinned and shook his head. "Aww, she sent a picture of her dog."

"What?" I snatched it away from him, but he was lying. It was a picture of Audrey. And she looked just like me.

6

"I can't believe how much you and Audrey look alike!" Dad said for the sixteenth time. "No one could mistake the fact that you're sisters, that's for sure."

I pushed the peas around on my plate. I just wanted the meal to end so that I could go up to my room.

"I mean, she has your green eyes . . . the same mouth . . . even the shape of your eyebrows are the same!"

"Don't forget that her hair is the same color as mine," interrupted Julian, his mouth full of mashed potatoes.

"It's rude to talk with food in your mouth!" I reminded him too sharply, and saw Dad look at me closely.

"Josey, everything okay?" he asked, his face concerned.

"I'm fine!" I snapped back. "Why is everyone asking me if I'm okay all the time?"

I pushed back my chair and rose from the table, picking up my plate and silverware even though it was Jake's night to clear. I could feel Dad's eyes on me, but he didn't say anything. I supposed he'd be coming to my room for a serious "talk" later.

On my way through the family room I saw Audrey's letter lying open on the side table, along with the infamous picture. Dad had set them there for Mom to read as soon as she got home, I knew. I picked up the letter and scanned the lines of neat handwriting.

I hope that you won't mind if I've chosen to write a letter rather than call on the phone. I'm really not much of a phone person and thought that by writing I'd have a better chance to think out what I wanted to say. Having said that, I'm as curious as you as to what I'm going to write next, since I've never written such an important letter before in my life.

When I began the search a few months ago I hoped that I'd be lucky enough to find one person—my birth mother. I had no idea that I'd be welcoming so many important new people into my life! To be completely honest, I'm not totally surprised, since my life has been filled from the beginning with happiness and good fortune. I was lucky enough to be adopted by two wonderful and loving parents, Louise and Truman Merriday, who after seven difficult years of trying to have children of their own, finally turned to adoption.

Two years after I arrived, my parents adopted another child, my brother Michael. Then, as often happens, my mother miraculously became pregnant not once, but twice, and so I also have two sisters, Kathryn and JoAnn, both of whom are now pursuing teaching degrees of their own. Michael is a Marine stationed on the West Coast, so we don't see him very often.

My parents were both teachers in the small town in western North Dakota where I was raised, and I lived there basically my entire life until I started college in Grand Forks. After seven years, I'm close to completing my doctoral training in psychology and am set to begin my internship at the Minneapolis VA Medical Center in a few weeks. While I'm excited at the prospect of finally beginning to practice as a psychologist, the one drawback of this final phase of my training is that it will mean that I have to spend a year away from my fiancé, Will. He's a terrific guy and I will certainly miss him, so I'm hoping that the next year will pass quickly.

Well, I'm kind of uncertain as to how to proceed from this point. I hope you understand if I tell you that I was a bit overwhelmed at the fact that there are so many of you. I am trusting, though, that good things will come to us all through the experience of getting to know one another.

The letter was simply signed "Audrey." I carefully refolded it and laid it back on the table, next to the picture of Audrey and Will. The photo appeared to have been taken at a formal event of some kind, judging by how they were dressed. Audrey was wearing a black dress, kind of sexy but not too over-the-top. It looked like a dress that both Sarah and Britt would approve of. Will, dark-haired, with a goatee, was a head taller than Audrey and had his arm around her in a comfortable way. Something seemed vaguely familiar about him, but it was hard to tell what, exactly, as his face was turned slightly to the side. I shrugged the feeling off, figuring I must be imagining things.

I studied Audrey's image again. The feeling of familiarity *there* was understandable; Dad hadn't been kidding when he said that there was a strong resemblance between us. Audrey had dark hair, though, and mine had always been blond. She didn't have my dimple in her right cheek, and she didn't look like Barbara Eden, but her smile was open and genuine. I wondered if she had to have braces, like I did.

The picture of Audrey both interested and bothered me, for reasons I couldn't put into fully formed thoughts. But those feelings were nothing compared to the way I felt when I read what Audrey had written in the fourth paragraph of her letter: *After seven years, I'm close to completing my doctoral training in psychology . . .*

Reading those words again gave me a stomachache.

I went upstairs and tried to focus unsuccessfully on my homework. Later, when I heard Dad's footsteps in the hall, I picked up the phone and pretended to be deep in a homework conversation with Sarah.

"Yeah? Well, what did you get for number seventeen? What?! How did you get that? Listen, if you take the second formula and apply it . . ." I waved my pencil cheerily at Dad, then covered the phone with my hand when he paused in the doorway. "Did you need me for something?"

"Um," Dad looked uneasy. "I thought we might talk for a couple minutes."

I pointed at my open book and grimaced apologetically.

"Geez, we're kind of in the middle of something here. Can it wait until later?"

He scratched his neck. "I guess so."

"Great, thanks." I uncovered the phone to resume my fake conversation. "What formula did you use for the one on page fourteen?" I asked the dial tone brightly.

After chatting to no one for a few more minutes just for good measure, I dialed the phone for real. Britt answered on the third ring.

"Speak."

"It's me."

Silence from the other end told me she was still mad at me. "Britt, I don't know what was wrong with me today. I really don't think you're dumb, not at all. And more importantly, you're my wonderful friend and I adore you, so won't you please forgive me? I've just kind of been . . . going through some things. You know."

Britt sighed heavily, "Alright, I accept your apology. But you and Sarah have to stop correcting me all the time."

"I promise," I said, without hesitation.

"Good." The tension on the line lessened considerably.

"So," I ventured, relieved that things were back to normal. "What are you doing?"

"Homework, what else? I don't know how they expect us to have a life if all we have time for is these stupid books! I mean we have a thousand years ahead of us to work, don't we?"

"Yeah."

"I suppose you're done with yours already," Britt pouted.

"No," I lied. "I've got tons left."

"So do I."

"Britt?"

"What?"

"We got a letter from Audrey today. You know, my surprise sister?"

"Ooh, what did it say?"

"She sent a picture. She looks a lot like me. Older, of course, but not as much as I expected. She has darker hair. And you know what else?" I paused, the words sticking in my throat.

"What?"

"She's a . . . psychologist."

"What?! Josey, that's incredible! It's like she's some kind of weird twin or something, only older. Wow, just think of how great that'll be; she'll be able to tell you all the right things to do to become a psychologist because she's already done them! You're so lucky. I wish I had an older sister who was a phlebotomy technician."

I considered this for a moment. Maybe Britt was right; maybe it *would* be a good thing to have an older sister who already was a psychologist. I imagined us a few years down the road, discussing our most challenging patients over coffee.

"Oh, Josey, you're so right," Audrey would say when I helped her formulate a case. "I wish I had your insights."

"Maybe you're right," I said to Britt. "Before you put it that way, I was kind of feeling bummed out that she was already a psychologist. You know, kind of like she stole my dream and made it happen before I got the chance to even try. But maybe it's really a good thing."

"Of course it is."

"Huh. Wow, Britt, you really *are* smart, you know that?"

"Mm-hmm. It's nice to finally be appreciated."

As I hung up the phone, I was actually feeling better. I got ready for bed, thinking about Audrey and imagining that maybe someday we'd even open a joint practice. "Muller and Merriday, Doctors of Psychology" we'd call it. Or how about "The Muller-Merriday Center for Self-Growth"? It was an exciting thought.

And yet later, when I heard my dad come back to peek into my room, I pretended like I was already asleep.

7

The next day was Friday. On the one hand, this was good, because I felt like the week had already been seventeen days long. On the less positive side, however, Fridays meant phys ed, which *this* time of year meant swimming lessons. I could never understand why the school thought that the chilly pre-winter months were a good time to have swimming, since the temperature outside was just cold enough to make our wet hair freeze into stiff clumps as we dashed across the street from the pool building to the high school after class.

One consolation was that Sarah, Britt, and I had somehow ended up in second-hour phys ed. If you had to stomp around in a swimsuit in late October, at least it was better to share the misery with familiar company.

"Ugh, I hate this suit," complained Sarah, struggling into her navy blue Speedo. "It's so hard to get on."

"I think they make Speedos tight like that on purpose," I pointed out. "Less water resistance so you can swim faster. You know, *Speed*-o?"

"The only thing I want to be speedy," Sarah replied, "is the next hour of my life."

Britt returned from the sinks, where she had been busy stuffing her long red hair into a white swimming cap. At the sight of her both Sarah and I burst out laughing.

"You look like half a Q-Tip!" Sarah told her.

Britt gave her a withering look. "Wait until you get yours on, sister."

"I don't know why they make us wear those things, anyway," I said. "Nobody looks good in them."

"I don't think the point is to look good," Sarah pointed out. "It's so we don't clog up the pool drains with our hair."

"Yeah, but won't the guys' hair clog up the drains too?"

"Hmm, that's a good point," Sarah narrowed her eyes. As a pre-attorney, she was always on the lookout for a good case to be made. She gave her suit one last tug, snatched up her swimming cap, and stalked out onto the pool deck.

When Britt and I arrived poolside, Sarah was already deep into a heated debate with the swimming coach, who looked as if he'd like to push her into the pool.

"I'm not going to go find eleven more swimming caps for the boys, if that's what you're saying," Coach Hagen was telling Sarah, an impatient expression on his face.

"Then the only thing you can do is let the girls go without caps too," she demanded, gesturing for emphasis toward Britt, me, and our Q-Tip heads. As if on cue, we both reached up and pulled off our rubber caps in a show of support.

"I'm sure you're aware that applying certain standards to one group and not to another on the sole basis of race, gender, or social status could be considered discrimination," Sarah told the coach seriously, her crossing her arms in disapproval.

Coach Hagen looked confused. "It's not on the basis of race, gender, or . . . whatever. It's on the basis of hair."

"But if you look around, Coach, you'll notice that there are lots of boys in this class with hair nearly as long as the girls. In some cases, even longer," she said, gesturing toward the shoulder-length mop of Davis Freeley, who looked like he wanted to crawl under the lifeguard bench.

"If you make only the girls wear caps, then that's clearly discrimination, and it's unconstitutional. I, for one, refuse to be treated this way, and I'm sure that the other girls in this class would agree with me."

There was a moment of silence, while Sarah and Coach Hagen stared each other down.

Finally, Coach Hagen shrugged. "Alright," he sighed, shaking his head. "No one has to wear swimming caps today. We'll revisit the issue after I talk to Principal Dawes."

He turned away from Sarah and blew his whistle shrilly.

"Enough wasted time," he shouted at the rest of us. "Everyone into the pool."

Sarah walked toward us, smiling triumphantly, "He's lucky he backed down," she confided. "Next I was going to threaten to schedule a press conference."

We congratulated her, threw our swim caps into the big storage bin outside the locker room, and jumped into the shallow end of the pool. Our happiness was short-lived, however; Coach Hagen's debate with Sarah had put him in such a foul mood that he made us swim laps the entire hour.

At lunchtime we were still trying to thaw out our hair.

"Man, I'm beat," whined Britt. "I don't ever want to see that pool again."

I nodded in weary agreement. "Me neither. And I have the worst brain-freeze headache ever."

Sarah was still warmed by her constitutional victory. "Yeah, but we stood up for what's right."

"I'll be surprised if by the end of the day I can stand up *at all*," Britt muttered under her breath.

I changed the subject. "What are we going to do this weekend?" I asked.

Britt considered. "You guys could sleep over. Maybe my dad would drop us off at the mall. We should start looking for something to wear to the Holidazzle dance."

"That's almost two months away," I reminded her. "Besides, have we decided whether we're all going together, or what?"

"You can count me in," Britt replied. Sarah was silent, and after a moment we both turned to look at her.

"Hmm?" she murmured innocently.

"Are we all going to the HOLIDAZZLE DANCE TOGETHER?" Britt and I chorused loudly.

Sarah looked embarrassed. "Good grief," she said, glancing around. "You don't have to yell. The thing is, well, I don't know. Someone sort of . . . asked me already."

Britt shot up straight in her chair. "What?" she hollered.

Sarah's face grew red. "Shhh," she scolded Britt. "I was in Study Hall yesterday and Josh Marto kind of asked me."

Britt and I were incredulous. "Uh, and you didn't bother to *mention* that to your best friends?" I demanded.

"Didn't I?"

Britt glared at her. *"NO, you didn't."*

"Oh . . . well, I thought I did. I guess maybe I forgot to bring it up." All of the bravado Sarah had shown at the pool that morning had melted away and she looked like she wanted to disappear with it.

"So?" Britt was relentless.

Sarah grimaced. "So . . . what?"

"So, are you actually *going* with him?" Britt and I both looked at Sarah accusingly.

"I guess so," Sarah whispered. Britt was silent for a moment, looking first at Sarah, then at me, then back to Sarah again. Suddenly a smile broke out on her face.

"Well, what do you know!" she crowed. "Finally one

of us has a date! I can't believe it!" Britt reached over to hug Sarah's neck. "Our little girl's becoming a woman!"

"Knock it off, you spaz," muttered Sarah, her face nearly purple.

"Do you know how much more fun it's going to be to shop dresses when one of us actually gets to wear ours on a real date?" I pointed out.

Sarah's cheeks were returning to their normal color, and she looked extremely relieved. "I just didn't know how you guys would react," she admitted. "So I never dared bring it up."

"Of course, we're really happy for you," I assured her, throwing an arm around her shoulders in a hug. I leaned close to her ear and said in a low voice, "But as your best friends, you do understand that it will be our duty to shout embarrassing things when you and Josh walk through the Holliberry arch."

Britt nodded seriously in mock agreement.

Sarah eyed me sideways. "What makes the two of you think that *you* won't have dates too?" she said.

"I'm not holding my breath," I scoffed. Britt brightened.

"Hey, maybe you could go with Charlie Goodall! He was kind of your knight-in-shining-armor yesterday, wasn't he?"

Now I was the one whose cheeks grew hot. I made a face at Britt to show what I thought of *that* idea, and elbowed Sarah a good one when she started laughing. But I was secretly pleased. I hadn't seen Charlie again after the fiasco outside of Algebra, but I had to admit that the way he stuck up for me had crossed my mind more than once.

"What about me?" wailed Britt. "Who's going to ask *me* to the Hollidazzle dance?"

"Why, Brandon Burke, of course," Sarah assured her. "The two of you can double date with Josey and Charlie!"

"Yeah, right!" Britt cracked up. "And someday I *will* be a rocket scientist!"

Sarah smiled. "Miracles do happen."

"Well, if we all get dates for the Hollidazzle, one will have happened," I reminded them. Britt bringing up the rocket scientist thing again made me nervous. "And I'm not holding my breath. Besides, I'll be just as happy to go with Britt."

"Me too," Britt smiled at me. "But even so, it's nice that one of us will be going with an actual date, even if it is just Josh Marto.

"No offense," she added, for Sarah's benefit.

8

When I got home from school I was surprised to find my mom curled up in the big chair in the family room, a pad of paper in her lap instead of the usual crossword puzzle. Crumpled-up balls of paper were scattered on the floor around her.

"Are you sick?" I asked with concern. I couldn't remember the last time my mom had taken an afternoon off from work for no reason.

"No," she smiled up at me. "I just wanted to write back to Audrey as soon as possible, and it was driving me crazy to be sitting at work with all the things I wanted to say running through my head."

"Oh." I couldn't help thinking that Mom had never taken a day off from work just because of me. To tell the truth, with all the excitement of Sarah's news I'd almost forgotten about the whole "Audrey" thing for a few hours.

"So, what have you written so far?"

She sighed. "Nothing that's any good, really. Her letter was, well, just so sweet and articulate, and I want to say exactly the right thing in my letter back to her. It's a lot of pressure to know that whatever I write will be the first words she hears directly from me."

"Yeah, I guess."

Mom bent over her paper again. I could see that she'd written about four lines, and crossed out two of them.

"Why don't you just tell her what happened; why you gave her up for adoption?" I suggested. "That's what I'd want to know if I were in her position."

"Yeah, I know. I've tried that in my previous attempts." She gestured at the floor. "But it comes out sounding kind of inadequate as far as explanations go."

"Maybe you're just over-thinking it," I told her.

Mom looked at me thoughtfully. "Maybe you're right," she said. She tore off what she'd written and crumpled it up. "Alright," she said, dropping it on the floor with the rest. "A fresh start. I'm just going to write and when I'm done, that'll be it."

"Go for it."

I left the family room and went upstairs to change. When I came down, Mom was writing steadily, her head bent over her pad.

"Mom?"

"Mm-hmm?" She didn't stop writing.

"Can I sleep over at Britt's tonight?"

"Hmm?"

I could tell she wasn't listening, so I decided to give her a few minutes. I went into the kitchen and took a bag of pretzels from the cupboard for a snack, and was pouring myself a glass of root beer when Jake came in.

"Hola," he greeted me.

"Burrito," I returned. "Hey, Jake, would you drop me off at Britt's later? I'm sleeping over there tonight."

"Sorry, *Señorita."* He grabbed a few pretzels out of the bag I had set on the table. "I've got a date."

"Yeah, but you can drop me off on your way."

"No can do," he said.

I glared at him. "Why do you have to be such a jerk all the time?"

"Who's a jerk?" asked Mom, coming into the kitchen. She was carrying a folded sheet of paper and looking pleased with herself.

"Jake won't drop me off at Britt's house," I told her.

Jake protested, "But I'm supposed to pick Lilja up at seven!"

"Why can't you drop me off on the way?"

Mom smiled at us both, which seemed odd, because she hates it when we bicker like this. "I can drop you off, honey," she assured me. "I've got to swing by the post office anyway and make sure this goes out in tonight's mail. Just let me hunt down some stamps."

Jake made a *haha* face at me from behind Mom's back. I was just about to flip him the bird when Mom turned back to me.

"Josey, could you ever do me a big favor?" Mom was holding the letter out to me. "Could you go over this and see how it sounds?"

I took the page from her and scanned it. As promised, she'd written straight through without even making any corrections or crossing anything out.

"Sure, I guess," I shrugged.

"While you're reading it, try to imagine, you know, that you're Audrey," she instructed me.

It will be a little difficult to imagine myself as someone I've never met, I thought, but I took the letter, along with my root beer, and went to sit down at the kitchen table.

Dear Audrey,

Like you, I'm finding this the hardest letter I've ever had to write. I can't tell you the joy you've brought to us by making contact, and I promise that we'll do everything within our power to make sure you feel comfortable with the process of getting to know us.

I can't imagine how shocking and confusing it must have been to find out that your search had resulted in a much different outcome than you'd anticipated. I'm sure the first question that comes to your mind is why we would choose to give up one of our children for adoption, then go on to have three more. Well, there's no easy answer to that difficult question. All I can tell you is that we were too young and too naïve when we conceived you, and the forces that controlled our lives at that time (namely, our parents) left us with little choice in what we had to do. It's not that we didn't love you; in fact we loved and continue to love you more than words can say. If there were any way to take back that decision I'd have done it every day since the day you were born.

It sounds as if you had wonderful parents, which eases my mind tremendously. I had imagined many possible outcomes to this situation, and none of them were as wonderful as you describe your parents to be. The strength and maturity reflected in your letter speak volumes about the way you've been raised, and I carry in my heart the utmost respect and gratitude for your parents.

In looking at your picture, I can see how much you resemble each of the other children in certain ways, Josey the most. You also share her interest in psychology; at almost sixteen she's trying to decide whether she wants to become a psychologist herself . . .

Mom went on to describe the boys, but I wasn't absorbing much after that. I was stuck on her comment that I was "trying to decide" whether to become a psychologist. Didn't she know how important becoming a psychologist was to me? Hadn't she been listening when I'd talked about going to graduate school after college? "Trying to decide" made me sound so juvenile, like I was some kid trying to figure out what to be when I grew up.

Mom ended the letter with, *We will proceed in whatever way and at whatever pace you feel most comfortable. We can hardly believe that we've been given this second chance to be in your life. Both David and I promise to do our best to be there for you in whatever capacity you wish. Thank you again for making this possible for us.*

She signed it, *Love, Anne.*

I folded the letter and laid it on the table as Mom came back into the kitchen. "So?" She studied my face in anticipation. "What did you think?"

"It's really good," I managed to squeak out around the lump of hurt in my throat. "I'm sure she'll like it."

"Great; I'm so relieved to have that done!" She took the letter from me and slipped it into an envelope she'd already addressed and stamped. "I can't wait to get it in the mail. Are you ready to head out?"

"But I can't go to Britt's until after dinner."

Mom was rereading her letter. She said absently, "Oh. Well, maybe I'll run to the post office myself. I can just give you a ride later; I'm just eager to get this sent off so it gets to Audrey by Monday."

I didn't respond, but Mom didn't seem to notice. She left the kitchen, inspecting the envelope's seal as if the letter might slip out of any available opening. I heard her take her jacket from the hall closet, then open the back door to the garage. A moment later, she was backing the car down the driveway and out into the street.

I was still sitting at the kitchen table when Jake came back. "You done with these?" he said, snatching the bag of pretzels off the table.

"You don't have to just grab them," I snapped at him in irritation. I swiped at the bag, even though I didn't really want any more pretzels.

Jake snickered and danced away out of my reach, digging his grubby hand into the bag to toss a few pretzels into his mouth.

"What's your problem, anyway?" he mumbled through a mouthful of crumbs.

"You."

I pushed back my chair and stomped out of the kitchen,and up to my room. Once there, I angrily pulled my overnight bag out of the closet and began stuffing things into it. Pajamas, slippers, underwear, jeans, and a sweatshirt for tomorrow. I didn't need to bring a sleeping bag, since the three of us always crowded into Britt's bed.

I was on my way to the bathroom to get my toothbrush when Jake came down the hall. "It's her, isn't it?" he asked. "That Audrey chick. It bugs you that you're not the only girl anymore."

I stared at him. Was he right? Is that why I felt so weird every time I heard her name?

"Wrong."

I couldn't let Jake think he was onto me, even if he was closer to the truth than he knew. An even *more* frightening fear had suddenly floated to the surface of my consciousness: What if Audrey was not only another daughter for my parents, but somehow a *better* one than I was? After all, she was clearly smart, maybe smarter than I was. God knows she was successful; she'd already achieved *my* primary goal in life. She even looked like me.

Was this why I felt as if a rock had taken up permanent residence in the pit of my stomach? Did I see Audrey as competition for the position that I thought was mine? I suddenly had a mental image of two people discussing our family.

First person: "Jake's sister Audrey is so smart and wonderful! I'm not sure what happened to the other sister."

Second person: "Other sister? Jake has another sister?"

First person (laughing scornfully): "Yeah, I think her name is . . . Janice or Julie or something like that. No one can ever remember."

I pushed past Jake and headed to the bathroom to grab my toothbrush, mentally giving myself a good shake. The whole idea was ridiculous, really.

Or was it? I thought of the words Mom had written, *We loved you and continue to love you more than words can say.* No one in my family really went around saying "I love you" to each other. It isn't that we don't feel it; we're just not the "I love you" kind of bunch. So it definitely felt strange to hear my mom say it to someone she didn't even know yet.

Thinking of the Audrey situation, I remembered that I'd meant to make some notes for my "nature versus nurture" project now that I'd seen a picture of her. I zipped up my overnight bag and found my psychology notebook. On the page where I'd written Audrey's name, I wrote a heading that read: "Physical Characteristics," under which I wrote *Hair: Brunette. Eyes: Green.*

It was hard to remember anything else about how Audrey looked, so I went to find the picture. It wasn't on the side table in the family room, and neither was her letter. A search of the family room and kitchen turned up nothing, and I finally ended up in my parents' room where I found the envelope with the letter lying on my mom's dresser. The picture, on the other hand, seemed to be missing. I was just about to give up when I glanced up at my mom's dresser and saw that she had tucked the picture inside the frame of the mirror, where she'd always displayed our most recent school photos.

Jake's, Julian's, and my pictures were still there, but the picture on the top of the order was no longer Jake's. Instead, the uppermost position now belonged to Audrey and Will, and the message it carried burned clearly in my mind. Within a matter of days, Audrey Merriday, a total stranger, had become the first and, in some odd way, the most important child in our family, and it was clear that none of the rest of us had anything to say about it.

9

By the following Wednesday, Mom had her answer; her letter to Audrey had been well-received. "She wrote back already!" Julian hollered from the family room when he heard me come in the back door.

I dropped my backpack and shrugged off my coat without saying anything. I had managed to put Audrey out of my mind for the weekend. Sarah had finally taken her driving test on Monday and passed, so now we had wheels. Britt, Sarah, and I had not found anything that we liked at the mall during the weekend, but when Sarah drove us there herself on Tuesday after school we had more success: we found a beautiful, shimmery blue dress at Nordstrom's for Sarah and a short, sparkly magenta one for Britt at Petite Teen.

Britt was ecstatic when she saw it. "It looks like it's

got snowflakes all over it!" she exclaimed. "What could be more perfect for the Hollidazzle?" It *was* perfect on Britt, who never believed that redheads shouldn't wear pink.

"Don't you think it's kind of bright?" asked Sarah doubtfully. "And maybe a little too short?" Her own ankle-length dress was conservative, like she was.

"Nope, it's just right," said Britt, admired herself in the mirror. "Don't you just love the little straps? Ooh, I'm going to have to get a tan."

In the end, even Sarah had to admit that the combination of Britt's hair, big brown eyes, and the striking pink dress was dramatic. Britt twirled and posed in front of the mirror, until we were all laughing.

"We didn't find anything for you, Josey," Sarah mourned as we left the mall with their bags.

"That's okay," I assured her. "The stores will be getting their Christmas stuff in soon, so there'll be even more to choose from."

The truth was, I was having a hard time focusing on the Holidazzle dance. It was taking too much energy not to notice that both of my parents seemed to be increasingly obsessed with Audrey. On the positive side, at least, I hadn't seen them act so in love in years. They couldn't pass each other in the hallway without smiling and reaching out to touch each other. At night they sat next to each other on the couch watching TV or playing Rummikub, and when I came down for water one evening I'd even caught them kissing.

Somehow, it seemed that the giddier they became, the

more gloomy I felt. I was annoyed with myself for being such a wet blanket, but I couldn't seem to cheer up.

As I knew it would, Audrey's quick response set off a flurry of excitement at our house. When Dad got home, he opened the letter even though it was addressed to Mom. I watched him read it out of the corner of my eye. He chuckled a couple of time, and once he said "No kidding" under his breath.

Finally he folded up the letter and put it on the side table for Mom. He was humming as he came into the kitchen to start dinner.

"So, she liked Mom's letter?" I couldn't keep myself from asking. I did not, I told myself, feel like reading Audrey's letter for myself.

"Yeah, she really liked it." Dad reached up into the cupboard above the stove and took down a box of angel hair pasta. "How about if I make that pesto dish that you like—the one with all the olives?"

"Sure."

"I'll have to call your mom and have her pick up some Italian bread." He was silent for a minute, thinking of what else he'd need. "And maybe some fresh basil."

"Does Mom even know what basil is?"

He grinned. "You're probably right. Maybe I can get by without it."

I watched him fill a pot with water and set it on the stove to boil.

"Want to chop the olives?" he asked. Dad knows I love

helping him cook. I'm kind of a natural at it, like he is; we can both just add this and that and end up with a dish that's pretty tasty. My mom, on the other hand, likes to joke that she can't cook toast. Frankly, she's right.

So I said "Sure," and Dad handed me two jars of olives, one green and one black. "Use the big knife," he instructed, gesturing toward the caddy where we keep our sharpest cutlery.

I drained the olives and piled them on the cutting board. It was difficult, at first, to keep them from rolling away from me, but after a few chops with the knife they stayed put.

It was soothing being in the kitchen with Dad, the big pot of water steaming on the stove and the salty smell of olives tickling my nose.

I was just starting to relax when Dad said casually, "So, it sounds like she's ready to meet us."

I started. "What? Who?"

Dad smiled over at me, looking really happy. "Audrey, silly! She said in her letter that she wants to figure out a plan to meet us."

"Oh." I swallowed hard, glad that my back was to Dad. "When?"

"Well," he came over to lean against the counter where I was working on the olives. "I was thinking that maybe it would be easier for her to meet just me and Mom first. Fewer people, you know?"

That was fine by me. "Okay."

"I know you're probably dying to meet her . . ."

"No, that's okay. I can wait." I tried to look sincere. "I mean, I want to meet her, of course, but I understand what you're saying about not wanting it to be overwhelming. I think you're right."

"Of course, we'll see what your mom says, but I was thinking that maybe she and I would fly to Fargo and stay overnight with Grandma and Grandpa Muller. Then we could drive to Grand Forks the next day and meet her and Will."

He'd already put a lot of thought into this, I realized. Suddenly something occurred to me.

"What will Grandma and Grandpa Muller think about this?" I asked. "I mean, weren't they the ones who made you give Audrey up for adoption?"

A furrow appeared between Dad's eyebrows. "Where did you get that idea?" he asked, sounding annoyed.

"Well . . . I guess Mom kind of described it that way."

Dad scowled. "Josey, your grandparents were just doing what they thought was best for me," he said. "Frankly, I think that they were forced into the position of making the difficult decision that *both* sets of parents probably favored. I don't think that they're any more responsible for the way things turned out than anyone else. And to answer your question, I've already phoned them and told them about Audrey's contacting us, and they're thrilled."

He got up and went over to check the water. I felt bad for upsetting him, but I was afraid to say anything else for fear it would be the wrong thing. When I finished chopping the olives, he brought me a bowl to put them in. He didn't seem annoyed anymore.

"Looks good, Josette," he said, inspecting my work. "Most people make a mess of that job." He smiled at me with his blue-green eyes. "I guess you must be taking after your old man."

I smiled at him. "You're not old."

"Depends on what day it is," he replied, as he always does. He studied my face, then shook his head. "I can't believe you're almost sixteen already."

I snorted. "I can't believe I'm not sixteen *yet*. Which reminds me; after I pass the Driver's Education course, can I get a car?"

He raised an eyebrow at me, Groucho Marx-style. "Let's not put the car before the course, young lady," he quipped, wiggling an invisible cigar.

"Very funny."

Dinner that night was especially tasty, due to candles Julian found for the table, Dad's skill with the pesto, and my perfectly chopped olives. Mom came home with a crusty loaf of Italian bread, as requested, and the delicious food put everyone in a good mood. Afterwards, drowsy with carbohydrates, I decided to turn in early.

"Goodnight, I'm going to bed," I informed my parents, who were sitting together in the family room. They were on the couch together watching *Whose Line Is It, Anyway?*, a show that always makes my dad laugh like crazy.

"Goodnight, sis, sleep tight," Mom waved at me, and my dad threw me a kiss. As I got to the bottom of the stairs I overheard Dad say, "You know, I think she's really handling all of this pretty well."

I took a few steps back toward the family room to listen.

"I mean, the boys seem fine, too," he continued. "But Josey's the one who's probably been affected the most."

"Do you think so?" Mom asked. "I was worried it was going to be Jake, being the oldest."

"Yeah, that's true, but we've got to remember that prior to a week ago Josey was pretty firmly entrenched in her position as our only daughter. Plus, Josey's much more of a thinker than the boys. She's been doing a lot of ruminating about all of this, you can bet."

"Hmm, you're probably right," Mom agreed, and I could imagine her nodding.

This was fascinating; I'd never heard my parents discuss me like this before. I was standing so still that my muscles were beginning to cramp. Plus, I realized, I was holding my breath. Carefully, I eased some air out of my lungs.

"Imagine what it will be like when they actually meet."

"I *can't* imagine it. Having all of our children together for the first time in life . . . I get choked up just thinking about it," Mom sounded like she was ready to cry at the very thought. "I hope I can hold it together."

The couch squeaked, and I suspected my dad had put his arm around Mom. "Don't worry, sweetheart," he soothed. "It will be nothing short of wonderful."

There was silence for a minute, and then I heard Dad ask, "Should I make some popcorn?" and Mom said "Sure," so I zipped up the stairs before my dad came out into the hall and caught me standing there, eavesdropping.

When I got to my room, I got out my "nature versus nurture" notebook and opened it to my page. *Thinker*, I wrote. It was the first word under the heading "Personality." It made me feel good to see it there.

10

The very next Friday my parents were on a plane to North Dakota to meet Audrey. Before they left, my mom packed and unpacked her suitcase a thousand times. I'd never seen her this unsure.

"It's colder in North Dakota than it is here," she told me. "You don't remember, but one year we spent Christmas with Grandma and Grandpa Muller in Fargo and I thought we were either going to die of dehydration inside their house or freeze to death outside."

"But didn't you *grow up* in Fargo?"

Mom chuckled. "Somehow it never seemed as cold back then. I guess when you live there it comes on gradually, so you just get used to it."

"What do you think of this?" She held up a navy blue sweater.

"How about your red turtleneck?" I suggested. "You always look great in red."

Mom screwed up her face in indecision. "Too bright, I think," she decided finally.

Ultimately, she settled on a chocolate brown crewneck sweater and her khaki pants. Brown always makes her eyes look especially sparkly. I noticed that aside from a few other clothing items and toiletries, the space in Mom's suitcase was mostly taken up by a giant family picture album.

"Maybe you aren't bringing enough pictures," I teased her.

Mom looked sheepish. "Audrey is going to want to see pictures of all of you, and I couldn't make up my mind which ones to bring, so I just brought them all. I could just kick myself for not sending pictures along with that first letter; I was so excited to get it in the mail that I never thought of it until I was driving away from the post office."

I picked up the navy sweater and refolded it for her. "So you're going to drive to Grand Forks on Saturday and spend the day?"

She nodded. "I talked to Will on the phone yesterday and he said that they'll be expecting us around noon. I hope it isn't too hard to find their house."

"Daddy can find it."

Mom surveyed her suitcase worriedly. "Well, I think that should about do it."

"Did you pack socks?"

"Oops, thanks for reminding me. In fact, I'd better bring extra."

As she lifted the socks from her dresser drawer I noticed that her hands were trembling.

"Mom, are you okay? Your hands are shaking!"

She sighed. "No . . . yes . . . I don't know. I guess I'm just nervous. What if it doesn't go well? What if she's actually really angry about all of this? What if—"

"Good grief, Mom, she doesn't sound angry in her letters."

"No, but maybe she's just being nice to reel us *in*, and then she's going to let us have it."

Her worried expression was so earnest that I couldn't help but laugh, and finally she laughed too. It was nice to be with her, talking like this, even if we were talking about Audrey. My mom's always at work, so I don't usually get much time with her, and it seemed like since Audrey had come into the picture she was even less available. Sure she might be home just as much, but it seemed like she was always talking on the phone, writing a letter to Audrey, or off somewhere brooding over a cigarette.

"La mama está loca," Jake had observed one day, watching my mom chuckling to herself over yet another letter she was working on. Because Audrey had some sort of aversion to talking on the phone, they had decided to stick to writing to each other until the actual meeting. Lately it seemed like a letter was either arriving or departing on nearly a daily basis.

"Your mother is just trying to make up for lost time," my dad pointed out one day when he caught me raising my eyebrows as I came across Audrey's latest letter in the mail. "Besides, the more we communicate with Audrey before we leave, the more comfortable the first meeting will be."

After Mom and Dad left for the airport, I spent several hours working on a paper for my Advanced English class. My author was Sinclair Lewis, and I had thoroughly enjoyed *Main Street*, so it was an easy essay to write.

Jake was supposedly in charge while my parents were away, and they'd given him strict instructions that we were to have no houseguests. He seemed to be under the impression that this restriction didn't apply to Lilja; within an hour after my parents' departure, they were lying on the couch in a tangle, watching movies they'd rented.

Jake was supposed to help keep an eye on Julian, but our kid brother was spending the night at his friend Ross's house, so he was no problem.

When I finished my paper I thought about calling Sarah, but remembered that she was probably busy with her AE assignment too. She'd been assigned Jane Austen and had to struggle through *Sense and Sensibility*. I decided not to interrupt her, figuring she'd call me when she was finished.

Britt, of course, was in regular English and had no essay to write. Instead, she was helping her mom paint the spare guest room in anticipation of Thanksgiving company. I decided to get something to drink and give her a call before starting on my paper proposal for psychology.

"You know we're not supposed to have guests in the house," I whispered pointedly to Jake when I passed through the family room on the way to the kitchen. Lilja had gotten up to go to the bathroom.

Jake made a face at me. "We're not doing anything wrong," he retorted. "Just watching TV."

"Still, Mom and Dad said no company," I folded my arms to emphasize my seriousness.

"Oh, get over yourself," Jake shot back sarcastically.

"Wow, impressive comeback," I congratulated him. "I'm just pointing out that Mom's probably going to wig out again if she finds out that Lilja was here while they were gone. Didn't you learn anything from that last episode, moron?"

Jake regarded me, attempting to gauge how dangerous I might be. "You better not rat me out, *rata.*"

"Call me whatever you want, *perdedor*. Which, in case you don't know, means LOSER!"

I emphasized my point by making the big "L" over my forehead. We both knew I wouldn't tell; I wasn't above threatening, but I wasn't a *rata* either.

Lilja returned from the bathroom and snuggled back into her spot against my brother. I rolled my eyes at him behind her back, knowing I'd made my point. Continuing into the kitchen, I grabbed a soda out of the fridge and called Britt.

It took her three rings to pick up the phone.

"Whassup?" I drawled, when she finally answered.

"Oh, hi," Britt said. She sounded out of breath. "Listen, I'm trying to talk my mom into doing a faux finish on the guestroom walls and she won't listen to me. Can I call you back?"

I shrugged. "Sure, no problem. Call me later."

That left me with no choice but to work on the proposal for my psychology project. It was due on Monday, although Mrs. Gasparini had already verbally approved my "nature versus nurture" topic. I trudged back to my room and began working on an outline for my proposal.

Both Jake and Julian were out on Sunday night when my parents arrived home wrapped in a blast of cold air from North Dakota. They were giggling like children when they came in the door.

"Oh, Josey, we had *such* a great time!" my mom bubbled, hugging me hello. Her words were tumbling over each other, and she seemed to be speaking in exclamation points.

"Audrey is . . . completely wonderful! You're going to love her; she's so much like you! We had no trouble finding their house; we just came down the street and it was right on the corner, and then, well, there they were!"

She stopped to take a breath. "Oh my goodness," she exclaimed apologetically. "I've had to pee ever since we left O'Hare!"

As she left to go to the bathroom, my dad gave me a hug too, and launched into his own version of events.

"It was so easy, Josey, not at all stressful. And the first

time we saw Audrey it was like she was, I don't know, *familiar*, somehow. I almost felt that I knew her already . . ."

He trailed off dreamily, lost in remembering the magical moment he first saw Audrey, I supposed. All of a sudden his face lit up. "Oh, and you'll never guess what! We came up with a great plan for how to get everyone together. Before Thanksgiving!"

My mouth went dry. "Before Thanksgiving? But that's in three weeks!"

"I know, I know, it's quick, but Audrey has to pack up and report to her internship in Minneapolis by the end of November, so she's squeezing us in as it is."

He chuckled. "Boy, I don't know how those two lovebirds are going to manage to be apart . . ."

"They're such an ideal couple," my mom agreed, returning from the bathroom. My parents smiled at each other, remembering, I supposed, how perfect Audrey and Will were. Looking at them, something in me suddenly snapped.

"Um, Jake had Lilja over here almost the entire time you were gone," I blurted. The words surprised me as much as they did my parents. I felt sick; there was no doubt that Jake was going to kill me.

Mom's smile disappeared from her face.

"But we specifically told him . . ." she began, then stopped and shook her head. She looked at Dad, the sparkle fading from her brown eyes. "I was hoping we could trust him with some adult responsibility while we were gone."

Dad took his coat off, looking suddenly tired. "Where is he now?"

"I don't know . . . at work, I think."

I wondered guiltily whether I should call Subway and tell Jake what I had done. It would be harder for him to kill me over the phone, and he could at least be prepared for what he would face when he got home.

Still, a deeper question was tugging at me: *What was wrong with me?* I wondered. *Why did I need to nip my parents' joy in the bud?*

I helped them carry their bags upstairs to unpack, but their good mood was spoiled and it was my fault. I went back downstairs and sat by myself in the family room, wondering if rather than becoming a psychologist, I needed to see one myself.

11

The next week flew by. I handed in my project proposal, which came back with a red "A" scrawled across the top and a note from Mrs. Gasparini.

"You've really got something unique and wonderful happening in your life," she wrote. "What an exciting time for your entire family!"

Yeah, *exciting*, I thought to myself, wondering whether that was exactly the right word. It seemed more like *draining* still applied. Sure I was excited to meet Audrey, but sometimes I couldn't help but think back on how much simpler life had seemed before the social worker had called us on that night in early October.

Take my mom, for example; ever since coming back from North Dakota she was always in a good mood, skipping around the house like she was a teenager instead of a forty-two-year-old woman. She'd gone out and bought some new clothes, and I'd even noticed that she had started wearing lipstick occasionally. And she was always on the phone, talking about Audrey to one of her friends or making arrangements for our upcoming trip to Cancun.

Yes, that's where our parents had decided we should meet our new sister: in Mexico.

"It'll be fun," said my dad, when he proposed the idea. "We all love Mexico, and we thought it would be great to be able to treat Audrey and Will to a fun vacation before Audrey leaves for her internship."

"Can I snorkel?" Julian wanted to know. He was the family fish.

Dad smiled. "Oh, I'm sure it can be arranged."

"Awesome!"

No one had to ask Juan Taco; it was a given that he'd be excited about a trip to Mexico.

Dad was looking at me. "Josey? What do you think?"

"Sure. Sounds great," I responded, mustering up as much enthusiasm as I could. In my fantasies I had always pictured myself meeting Audrey in Woodridge, maybe at our house or in an office somewhere, with a social worker looking on approvingly. "But why don't they just come here?"

"Well, we considered that," Dad explained. "But in the end we just decided that it would be better for the meeting to take place on neutral territory. Audrey's very nervous, you know."

"Hmmm." Didn't it matter to anyone where the *rest* of us might be most comfortable? Not that I was nervous, exactly, but still . . .

As if she could read my mind, Mom tried to reassure me. "Daddy and I just thought that if we met in a beautiful, exotic place there would be things for us all to see and do while we get acquainted. I think it will make things more relaxing all around. And besides, I was able to arrange for Audrey to fly on my family flight benefits."

"But don't you have to be an actual family member for that?"

The words were out of my mouth before I could stop them.

Mom didn't seem bothered by my comment. "Well, Audrey *is* part of our family, and even though we'll have to pay for Will, I was able to get a discount for him as her fiancé. I had to explain the whole thing to Human Resources, but they went for it. So what do you think?"

"Can we go back to Puerto Vallerta?" I was remembering a particularly cute waiter who had smiled at me during dinner one night.

"Actually, we thought we'd try Cancun this time," my dad said, dashing my daydream. "This way everything will be new to all of us and we can experience it together."

In theory, it sounded pretty good, but there was a nagging feeling tugging at the back of my brain. I tried to interpret it: *Happiness?* Mmm, not exactly. *Excitement?* Well, maybe something in that neighborhood. *Fear?*

Suddenly I realized Dad was watching me. "What?" I said, more defensively than I meant to.

"Uh . . . well, I know you hate being asked this, Josey," he said finally. "But . . . "

I gave him my best "it's all good" face. "I'm *fi-i-ine*," I stretched out the word, bugging my eyes at him in an exaggerated fashion. "I was just thinking about what to pack."

I could tell he wanted to be reassured, so he let himself be. "You're just going to love Audrey," he repeated for the eight hundredth time in a week.

"Yep."

"You two have so much in common."

"Yeah, like our *parents*."

Dad gave me a patient look. "More than just that. You're both sweet and funny, and you look alike, and—"

"That may be," I interrupted, attempting to lighten things up. "But does she have the Muller toes?"

Jake, Julian, and I all have my dad's toes; they're so long that we like to tell people they're not *really* toes, they're extra fingers.

He laughed. "Hmm, well, that topic never came up when we were in North Dakota. Don't worry, I'm sure she'll be wearing sandals when we're in Mexico, and we can check it out then to see if she's a *real* Muller."

Dad was looking at me so warmly that I thought about bringing up the "nature versus nurture" project, but just then the phone rang. "I'll get it!" I volunteered. I knew an escape opportunity when I saw one.

At school, I told Britt and Sarah about the trip. "I can't believe you're going to Mexico!" wailed Britt. "You're always so lucky!"

"Yeah, I guess."

Sarah regarded me closely. "So this is finally it, huh? You're going to meet her?"

"Mm-hm." I was working hard to appear nonchalant, with apparent success.

"Wow." Sarah looked impressed. "Well, just make sure you take lots of pictures."

"Don't worry; I'm sure my mom and dad will be taking *plenty*."

"Are you nervous?"

I nodded. I could admit this to Sarah. "A little," I told her.

I noticed Britt had dropped out of the conversation and was eyeing my sweater. It was an old one of Jake's and a little stretched out. Okay, it was *really* stretched out.

"What are you going to bring for clothes?" she asked finally.

"Oh, I don't know," I shrugged. "The usual, I suppose. Shorts and T-shirts. A couple of swimming suits. Casual stuff."

Britt opened her mouth to say something, and then closed it again.

"Something on your mind?" I asked suspiciously.

She chewed her bottom lip. "Well, no."

"You'd better just tell me, because you're a bad liar."

Britt sighed. "It's just that . . . well, you want to make a good impression, don't you?"

"Obviously."

"So maybe you should update your look a little. Buy a few new things."

Sarah exhaled impatiently. "Britt, she's just going to be lying on the beach in Mexico. It's not like she needs to be the height of fashion." She patted my arm reassuringly. "I'm sure you'll know what to bring."

I wasn't so sure, suddenly. The night before, I had surveyed my wardrobe with the same general question in mind. Usually when we went someplace tropical I traveled light, taking only what I could fit into a backpack. A swimming suit, a couple T-shirts, a couple pairs of shorts, and a pair of sandals usually meant that I was good to go. It was all I needed, since our family is not the sort that goes out for fancy dinners.

Most of my summer things had already been packed away for winter, but I'd found my favorite pair of cut-offs on the floor of my closet. They had missed being stored away with the other summer clothes because I'd worn them up until the last minute. Even I had to admit that the cut-offs *were* looking pretty dingy. I'd stacked them and a few other things on top of my desk, and told myself I'd think about it later.

"What exactly do you think I need?" I asked Britt now. To tell the truth, I was kind of grateful to have the input.

"Well," Britt began eagerly, "some new shorts, at least.

Those cut-offs were looking awfully tired last time I saw them. A couple cute tops. Or maybe some little summer dresses . . ."

I made a face, picturing my brothers' reactions if I suddenly started showing up in little summer dresses.

"I don't really think that's me. Plus, where am I going to find little summer dresses in November?"

Britt shrugged, looking injured. "I don't know. It was just an idea," she said.

To tell the truth, the conversation had gotten me thinking. Of course I wanted Audrey's first impression of me to be a good one. In fact, I wanted it to be a *really* good one. The shorts had probably seen better days. And maybe a casual skirt wouldn't be such a bad idea . . .

"Can you meet me at the mall on Saturday?" I agreed reluctantly. Although I loved shopping, buying things for the trip to Mexico made meeting Audrey seem all the more real.

Britt sat up. "One-thirty sharp in the food court," she instructed me.

"Okay. I'll be there."

"You'll have to go without me," Sarah said. "I have an extra violin lesson on Saturday." Sarah played with the Woodridge City Orchestra, and they had the Holiday Music Festival coming up.

"So," she said, looking at me. "What are you going to say to her, do you think? You know, the first time you meet her."

I hadn't considered this. I looked at my friends blankly. "I don't know. What should I say?"

"Maybe something like, 'I'm honored to meet you,'" suggested Britt.

Sarah snickered. "She's not meeting the Queen of England, for cripes' sake."

Britt made a face at her and sat back, crossing her arms. "Well, what do you think she should say then, if you're so smart?" she demanded.

"I don't know. How about something like . . . 'I'm happy to meet you,' or 'I'm glad to know you.' Not too formal."

They both looked at me expectantly.

"Actually, I was just thinking of saying 'Hi, I'm Josey,'" I said, knowing suddenly how weak it sounded.

Sarah shook her head dismissively. "No, that's not good enough. After all, Josey, whatever you say is going to be the first words you ever speak to your sister. I mean, it's probably a moment that you will both remember for the rest of your lives."

I hadn't thought of it that way. Boy, I was feeling less and less like getting on that plane to Mexico with every passing second.

"Well, it's a good thing that there's no pressure or anything," I sighed.

Sarah was caught up in the fantasy now. "I suppose she'll hug you and maybe cry, like they do on TV."

While I was entertaining this alarming possibility, Britt said thoughtfully, "I can't believe she hates talking on the phone." Sarah and I nodded in agreement; it was hard to imagine being someone who didn't enjoy talking on the phone.

Truthfully, though, it was secretly a relief to know that I didn't have to worry about picking up the phone one day to find my new sister on the other end. I was afraid I might freeze up, or say something dumb that I couldn't take back. Of course, these same things might happen just as easily in person, but somehow I felt that it was less likely.

"By the way," Sarah said, changing the subject. "We can't forget that we still haven't found you a Hollidazzle dress."

I nodded. "Yeah, I know."

The Holidazzle dance had become a distant concern in the drama of the upcoming trip to Mexico. I wished that the date of the dance were here; it would mean that the meeting was behind me and I would be able to look back and know whether or not it had gone well. Hopefully, by that point I'd be feeling great about my new sister, Audrey. We'd probably be calling back and forth every night because I'd be the one person she felt comfortable talking to on the phone.

Britt thought. "When exactly do you leave again?"

"On the 5th, and come back on the 9th."

"Well, we'd better hit the stores right after that. We don't want to be left with nothing to pick from."

"Right."

So far Britt and I were still each other's dates for the dance. I suspected that was about to change, however.

Johnny Hudson had leaned toward me in Biology earlier in the week, and, after much fidgeting and throat-clearing, had asked in a casually strangled voice, "So, is your friend Britt going to the stupid Holidazzle dance with anyone?"

He flipped his long, dark hair out of his eyes with a quick shake of his head. Johnny was a nice guy, but always desperately in need of a haircut.

"Um, so far she's just going with me," I replied, feeling suddenly depressed. An image crept into my head of me home alone eating popcorn and watching music videos while everyone else was having fun at the Holidazzle dance.

Johnny didn't appear too concerned about the prospect of my having a boring evening at home. In fact, he looked thrilled.

"Great!" he said, giving his hair another flip.

Great, I echoed to myself.

Saturday I managed to get Jake to drive me to the Woodlake mall by begging his forgiveness for the Lilja incident and offering to make his bed for two weeks. I also had to promise, against my better judgment, to cover for him the night of the Hollidazzle while he and Lilja went into the city to see a show and have dinner.

"It's not like we're doing anything bad or dangerous," he said. "But you know how Mom and Dad are; they'd never go for it."

"Well, why do you have to do it at all? Why can't you just go to the dance like everyone else?"

"We're seniors; we're getting too old for that kid stuff,"

he replied. "And Lilja says she wants to have a real date in the city. I just need you to say you saw us at the dance if Mom or Dad asks. You don't even have to bring it up unless they do. And maybe you could also say you that you ran into us later at a party or something."

"What if they check the mileage on the car?"

It was at least sixty or seventy miles miles into the city and back, including driving around.

"They won't. Besides, we'll be back by one or two. They won't care as long as I'm home before dawn."

He gave me his most winning smile. "Don't worry, Josey, nothing's going to happen. We'll just drive in, have dinner, see the show, and come back."

"Okay, but I better not end up with someone calling me 'Auntie,' if you know what I mean."

Jake snorted, which didn't make me feel completely reassured. Actually, I wasn't even sure why I cared. If he and Lilja were stupid enough to produce a *bambino* before he graduated from high school, then that was his problem. Maybe it was kind of a family tradition.

I was glad Britt could meet me at the mall for a fashion consultation. It wasn't that I didn't value Sarah's opinion in matters relating to style, but Britt really loved clothes. Back when we were all still playing Barbies together, Britt's was the doll dressed in the funky downtown outfits, while Sarah and I unimaginatively paired the yellow slacks with the yellow shoes and the yellow top.

"Okay, I've already scoped out a few places," she said

breathlessly, spotting me as I approached. "Now I know that you usually like to get your stuff at Gap and Abercrombie, but I also think we should check out Contempo Casuals just to see what they have . . ."

"Uh, that place is a little over-the-top for me." I could just picture myself meeting Audrey in some kind of hip-hugging J.Lo ensemble.

She gave me an exasperated look, "Josey, do you want to look boring, or do you want to look amazing?"

"Somewhere in between."

"Then you've just got to trust me. I know what I'm doing here."

I sighed. She was right, and we both knew it.

"Okay. But I'm not wearing anything that's not completely comfortable," I warned her.

"Fine. Trust me."

She linked her arm through mine and gently led me out of the food court. "Maybe we should start with someplace that's fairly mainstream, but that still has some style," she said, more to herself than to me. She stopped suddenly and held up a finger, inspired. "Aha," she said. "Express."

In Express, Britt darted around like a hummingbird, gathering a heaping armload of clothing. She pushed me into a dressing room. "Try these," she instructed, transferring the clothes from her arm onto the hooks on the wall. "I'll be back with more."

I dropped the three things I'd managed to grab myself onto the upholstered bench, and then realized that they looked exactly like things I already had at home. Better to start with Britt's choices, I reasoned, since she was going through all this trouble on my behalf. Besides, maybe it was time for something different.

I cast a dubious eye toward a colorfully striped halter top, and noted the big silver ring decorating the front. It was too late to complain; Britt was already across the store, flipping through the racks.

"Do you have this zebra print in a small?" I heard her ask someone.

I sighed and changed into the top. It was a little *too* colorful for me, I decided, looking at myself in the mirror. The pattern almost hurt my eyes, and I didn't like the way the silky polyester felt against my skin. I pulled it off, shivering, and hung it back on its hanger.

Britt reappeared with another pile of clothes. "Didn't work for you?" she asked, eyeing the top. "Yeah, maybe the stripes are a little too much."

I tried on a few items for her, and she quickly rejected them as too tight, too loose, or too boring. She threw the tops that I'd selected into the "too boring" pile without even letting me try them on.

"Try that one," she instructed, pointing at a thin, scarf-like blouse that was falling off its hanger. It was not something that I would've chosen on my own, but I pulled it over my head and checked myself out in the mirror.

"Wow! I think we've finally found something!" exclaimed Britt.

I had to admit it wasn't bad. There was no doubt I looked different from how I usually looked. More interesting, like some kind of hippy-Bohemian flower child.

"It's great . . . you look at least seventeen in it," Britt assured me, reading my mind. "We're getting *that* one for sure."

I didn't feel strongly enough about it to argue, so I took my new blouse off and hung it up carefully.

We didn't find anything else at Express. I grudgingly accompanied Britt into Contempo Casuals, where I refused to try on the pair of lavender pleather jeans.

"Oh, come *on*," she begged me. "You'd be hot in these!"

"Exactly," I pointed out. "I'm not going for hot. I'm going for cool."

She gave me a look. "Well, *I'm* going to try them on then," she said, grabbing her size and flouncing off toward the dressing rooms, where a salesgirl unlocked the door for her.

I sank down onto the fuchsia fun-fur chaise in front of the dressing area, my lone blouse in a bag on my lap. Shopping with Britt could be exhausting, I reflected. The constant low hum of the mall environment drained me. Britt, on the other hand, was like a rechargeable battery leaching energy from the neon storefronts we passed.

"What do you think?" she threw open the door of her dressing cubicle.

"Wow."

"Don't you love them?" she swiveled around to check

out her lavendar-clad behind in the mirror. From my seat on the chaise, I could hear the pleather squeak. "I'm definitely getting them."

"Aren't they awfully tight? They look uncomfortable."

"They're supposed to be tight," Britt informed me dismissively. "And anyway, sometimes you have to sacrifice comfort for style."

"Hm."

In my book, there was almost never a good enough reason to sacrifice comfort, but I knew better than to say it out loud. And the truth was, Britt could carry off "style" in a way that I never could.

Her new pleather-wear put Britt in such a good mood that I was able to steer her into Gap without a fight. There she allowed me to buy two pairs of not-too-boring and not-too-uncomfortable shorts off a rack of summer clearance items. "But you have to try this too," she insisted, holding up a green paisley print summer dress.

I fingered the cotton material. "Hmm, I don't really know if it's me."

"At least try it on," Britt urged. "You have to try on the shorts anyhow."

"Alright." I agreed finally. The dress felt light on the hanger and I had to admit that it would be the perfect weight for the warm weather of Mexico. And it was my size, to boot.

After I confirmed that the shorts fit fine, I hesitantly slipped the dress over my head. In the mirror I could see right away that the green pattern brought out the green in my eyes and made my hair look even more blond. The dress fit perfectly and the cotton skirt felt good brushing against my legs. I opened the door to show Britt.

"Oh . . . my . . . gosh; it's *fabulous!*" she raved. "You look amazing!"

I nodded. "I actually love it."

I couldn't stop looking at myself in the mirror. Even I had to admit that I looked terrific. "I can wear my green peridot earrings with it," I said. "The ones my parents gave me for my birthday last year."

"And you have to wear my strappy sandals." Britt's voice rose with the exhilaration of an outfit well-planned.

We grinned at each other, thrilled at the success of our shopping efforts.

"Okay, take it off so we can get out of here," Britt urged. "I'm starving!"

Closing the door, I couldn't resist looking at myself in the mirror a moment longer. It was exactly the right thing, I could feel it. Maybe I was finally prepared to meet Audrey after all.

12

Before I knew what hit me, the week of the fifth was here and we were headed to Mexico. My mom had arranged it so that we would arrive a day before Audrey and Will, to settle in and make sure everything was okay for their arrival. Honestly, you'd have thought we were going to be entertaining royalty, Spanish-style.

Flying makes me a little queasy, so Dad brought home some Dramamine from the pharmacy. It always makes me sleepy, but this time it really hit me hard; I closed my eyes as we took off in Chicago and the next time I opened them our plane was hitting the ground in Cancun. I didn't even remember changing planes in Miami.

When I woke up, my mouth was cottony and the shoulder of my T-shirt was wet, telling me that I'd been drooling like an idiot for God only knows how long.

"Hey, I got a couple of *great* pictures of you," Jake informed me as we disembarked into the Yucatan heat. "I'm thinking the kids at school might be interested in hearing about our trip . . . and seeing the photos, of course."

He jumped back to avoid my half-hearted punch. I knew he was still a little mad at me about ratting out him and Lilja to our parents, and I didn't really blame him.

The airport in Cancun was typical by Mexican standards, meaning that it was basically a plain concrete building sitting out in the middle of a field. Dad tracked down the bags, while Mom smoked a cigarette before she started negotiating for a rental car. We were practically going to need a bus to manage the seven of us, including Audrey and Will once they arrived.

I watched Mom inhale her cigarette like she was starving and it was a bacon cheeseburger. That's the hard part about traveling for her; she can't smoke. I knew she was nervous too, the way she'd been darting around like a fidgety little bird before we left. She'd worked her way through so many cigarettes on the way to the airport that my dad finally gave her a look. "What?" she snapped, when she saw him glance at her. Even though I was in the back seat, I'd felt the tension stretch between them like a wire. I had braced myself for an argument but it never happened; after a moment my dad just turned back to the road and Mom lit up.

Somehow she'd made it through the flight and we could all breathe a sigh of relief now that we'd finally arrived in Mexico. "Boy, you were really sleeping during the flight," Julian said to me, smiling. "I tried to wake you up to play cards, but you wouldn't even open your eyes."

"Yeah, the Dramamine knocked me out."

Jake was sitting on top of his duffel, watching Mom finish her cigarette. I figured he was probably wishing he could have one too, but he'd have to suffer. My parents would have a coronary if they thought either one of us had touched cigarettes.

Instead he looked over at me. "Nice look," he grinned, nodding toward the wet spot on my T-shirt. "Maybe next time you should ask for a drool bib."

I glanced over to make sure my mom was still occupied with her cigarette, then quickly flipped up my middle finger at him. Just my luck; Mom's radar was up.

"Josey, you know I don't appreciate that."

"Well, he was being a jerk . . ." I protested feebly.

Mom stubbed out her cigarette in the miniature ashtray built into the arm of her chair. I noticed she had dark smudges under her eyes, as though she hadn't gotten a good night's sleep.

"Listen, all of you," she said, regarding the three of us. "This weekend is going to be a really important one for us all. And when I say that, I mean it's a really, *really* important one. I would appreciate it if you would all try and act like mature young adults so that things can go as smoothly as possible. Can we agree on that, at least?"

"Yes," Julian and I chorused dutifully, and Jake shrugged with what passed for agreement. His attention had already been diverted by a group of three girls passing by, their dark hair shining. They were talking and laughing; I suddenly missed Britt and Sarah terribly.

My dad came back pulling the two big suitcases that contained my parents' clothes and other things my mother had felt were essential to bring along. It was highly unusual for us to actually check baggage; generally my parents travel almost as light as we kids do, and we're able to carry on all our belongings.

One philosophy my parents have about traveling is that if you're going to visit a new place, you should try to absorb as much of the true regional flavor as possible. Consequently, we generally bypass the popular tourist hotels and restaurants in favor of smaller, locally owned establishments. My mom is a genius at finding these places, so we've eaten authentic Jamaican cuisine in Negril and stayed in a grass-thatched hut with no running water in Costa Rica. In Puerto Rico, Jake, Julian, and I slept right on the beach, although when my mom found out the next morning she had a fit.

On past trips to Mexico, we'd rented one of the many *casas* available year-round. My mom had *really* gone all out this time, I realized as we drove up to what could only be described as a compound. Passing through the iron gates, I caught a glimpse of the Gulf of Mexico sparkling in the distance behind our sprawling villa. White stucco walls and curving doorways provided a dramatic contrast to the lovely blue lines of the horizon.

"Wow!" Even Julian, riding in the back seat, was impressed.

"Do you think they'll like it?" my mother asked anxiously. "I don't know; it seems so *big*. I was hoping for something a little cozier."

"It couldn't be better," my dad assured her, reaching over to touch her shoulder. I, too, murmured that it was great. Jake was too busy staring out the window at the surf, biting on a hangnail. From this angle I noticed what looked like a faint hickey at the base of his neck. Apparently Lilja had wanted to mark her territory before he left. I filed the information away for blackmailing purposes.

Dad pulled the Suburban up in front of the villa and we all climbed out into air that was warm and heavy with humidity. Just carrying the bags to the house sent a river of sweat coursing down between my shoulder blades; it was a delightful sensation to open the door and be welcomed by a current of cool air. As my eyes adjusted, I realized the place wasn't even air-conditioned; like many homes in Mexico this one was open to the outside, and the natural cooling effect was the result of shade, glazed tiles, and slowly circling ceiling fans stirring the air.

Inside, the house was lovely. At one end of the expansive great room, heavy furniture made of dark, Mediterranean wood was scattered casually around a large sisal rug. Aztec-patterned cushions softened the effect, and the white plaster walls were the perfect backdrop for colorful folk-art pieces. We had learned about Aztec folk-art in Spanish class, and I had always been fascinated by the contrast of bright, joyous colors and dark, sinister images portrayed by the figures themselves. The statue nearest me, for example, was half-animal, half-witch, representing a *nahual,* or a "good spirit which had gone bad."

At the other end of the room stood an enormous dining table made of dark, smooth wood, with ten high-backed chairs arranged around it. The dining area opened onto the kitchen, and from that portal a rotund woman suddenly bustled, her shining black hair streaked with gray. She nodded at us cheerily but continued on her way, retrieving a stack of dishes from a buffet and carrying them back into the kitchen.

"That must be the housekeeper," commented my mother. "The travel agent said that staff comes with the house. She'll be preparing meals for us and taking care of the rooms. I doubt she speaks much English, though; most of them don't."

Hearing this, Jake perked up next to me. I seriously doubted the poor woman would be getting much of her work done if my brother intended to practice his Spanish on her all day long.

We spent the next few hours unpacking and exploring before sitting down to a delicious dinner. Our housekeeper, who introduced herself as Marisol, had prepared a delicious beef stew made with chili peppers, tomato, cumin, and garlic.

"Carne guisada," nodded Marisol proudly, when my

mom complemented her on the dish. "I make this for *mi familia*."

"*Delicioso,*" enthused my father, causing Jake to roll his eyes in embarrassment.

"Delicio*sa*," he corrected.

Turning to Marisol, he questioned, *"¿Usted es buen cociner? ¿Usted tiene hijas?"*

"What did he say?" Dad asked. His command of Spanish is pretty limited.

"I didn't catch it," I lied, cutting my eyes at Jake. I guessed I owed him one.

"He asked her if she has any daughters!" supplied Julian helpfully. Apparently seventh-grade Spanish class was paying off. At least Jake had the decency to look embarrassed; this time it was my mom who rolled her eyes.

The next morning my parents left for the airport immediately after breakfast. Audrey and Will would be arriving on the 11 a.m. flight, and my mom didn't want them to have to wait around in a strange Mexican airport. I saw Marisol looking concerned as she cleared away the breakfast dishes. Neither my parents nor I had eaten much.

"*¡Desayuno delicioso!*" I assured her, smiling and gesturing toward the remains of the *huevos rancheros* she had made. Normally I like eggs, but my stomach hadn't felt ready for spicy food that morning, and I certainly didn't want to be in the bathroom when Audrey and Will made their entrance.

Jake sauntered into the living room, his hair wet from the shower. "I think I'm going to go look for the public beach," he informed me.

"What?" I was shocked. "Mom and Dad will be back by lunchtime with Audrey and Will! Don't you want to be here?"

Jake considered this, then sighed heavily. "I guess I could wait awhile." He plopped onto the sofa and put his feet up on the coffee table.

"What's for lunch?" he called to Marisol in Spanish, *"¿Cuál está para el almuerzo?"*

She gave him an approving look and launched into a long and enthusiastic description of the feast she'd be serving us in a mere three hours. Jake listened raptly, as if he hadn't just polished off several platefuls of eggs, cheese, and chiles.

"¡Grande!" he enthused when she was finished, giving her a big thumbs-up. Anyone in America would have thought he was being a smart-ass, but Marisol looked pleased.

"What?" he demanded, when he noticed the sour look on my face.

"How can you even *think* about eating?" I asked him, exasperated. "First of all, you just ate a disgusting amount of food, and secondly, aren't you at all *freaked out?"*

Jake raised his eyebrows as if he had no idea what I was talking about. He reached up to run his fingers absently through his damp hair, his version of a comb. "About them coming here today?"

I nodded hopelessly. What *else* could I have possibly meant?

Jake considered, and for a minute I thought he was going to tell me that he was just as unnerved by the prospect of meeting Audrey as I was. But I should've known better; Jake and I are two different animals.

"Nah," he said finally. "Maybe I was a little weirded out when I first heard about the whole thing, but now I'm used to it. What's the point of being freaked out?"

"No *point*," I sputtered in frustration. "A person can't change how they feel just because their feelings do or do not have a *point!*"

I realized too late that my voice sounded louder and more hysterical than I'd meant it to. Jake laced his hands behind his head and stared at me.

"The only thing I know is that *you're* freaking me out!" he said, and started laughing like a monkey.

I gave him a withering look. "I just hope that you can grow up in the next hour and a half so you don't embarrass our entire family."

"Oooh," he returned, waving both hands in front of him in mock terror.

I realized too late that it was obviously a waste of time trying to have a mature talk with my older brother, so I went to the veranda to get some sun. Stretching my legs out in front of me I was pleased to notice how smooth and tanned they already looked against the light green cotton of my dress. It was the new paisley dress, the one I'd bought when I was shopping with Britt. Putting it on that morning, I'd immediately felt more confident, and now I wished with all my heart that Britt and Sarah were here on the veranda with me, sipping icy glasses of Diet Coke and catching some rays.

A few minutes later Julian joined me.

"Look what I caught," he said, opening his hand to show me a tiny green lizard. "Marisol says it's not dangerous."

I regarded the lizard, which was about the size of a praying mantis. "Even *I* could've told you that. It's cute."

"Yeah." He set the lizard down on the patio; the cement was already warm from the morning sun and the lizard sat motionless for a moment before gamboling off into the grass. It didn't seem to think we were especially dangerous either.

Julian regarded me. "You look nice," he observed.

"Do you think so?" I smoothed the skirt of my dress over my knees and looked at him gratefully. "I don't look too . . . dressed up or anything?"

"No, you look good," my favorite brother assured me.

He paused thoughtfully. "It's weird, huh? Meeting a sister we've never met, I mean."

"Yeah, it's weird." I was relieved to know that I wasn't the only one feeling apprehensive. "What do you think she'll be like?" I asked him.

Julian shrugged. "I don't know. Like our parents, I guess. I mean, she's already a grown-up, right?"

I reflected on this, looking out over the horizon. The wind was up, creating whitecaps among the sparkling waves. "She's a pretty young grown-up though; only a few years older than Jake."

"Oh." He was quiet for a moment, thinking.

Finally he asked, "Are we supposed to . . . d-d-do you

think we should hug her?" Julian looked so nervous I had to smile.

"No," I assured him. "I don't think that we have to hug her. After all, we're all basically strangers; she probably wouldn't feel comfortable hugging us either."

Julian looked relieved. "Okay. Good."

I sat up. "Do you know if there's any Diet Coke in the fridge?" The conversation had left me feeling dry.

He didn't, so I went to find out for myself. There was, thankfully, and when I popped the can's top the familiar hiss of escaping carbonation felt like a message from my old, normal life telling me that everything was going to be all right. It was good timing, too, because just then I heard the front door open.

"Hey, everyone!" Mom called. "We're here!"

14

Looking back, the next few minutes were a blur, and yet something I'll probably remember for the rest of my life.

I set down my Diet Coke and came out of the kitchen, ready to meet my sister. She and Mom were still near the front door, which was standing open, giving me a view of Dad and Will outside, lifting suitcases from the back of the vehicle.

"Josey," Mom said, her voice proud. "This is your sister, Audrey."

Before I could say anything, Audrey was across the room and had her arms around me in a hug.

"You're even prettier than in your pictures!" she smiled, two inches away from my face. Up this close, I could smell her light, flowery perfume, and see that her eyes weren't really green after all; they were closer to my dad's aquamarine color. She was smaller than I'd imagined too, close to Julian's size, even though she was wearing a pair of platform sandals that would have definitely earned Britt's approval.

Audrey's dark hair was caught up in a neat ponytail, and she was casually dressed in shorts and a cotton blouse that looked freshly pressed, in spite of the long plane ride. *She barely looks older than Jake*, I thought.

"Hi," I said, realizing that I hadn't spoken yet. "It's really good to finally meet you."

Now see, that came out sounding fine, I thought with satisfaction, and made a mental note to tell Britt and Sarah.

"How was your trip?" I asked politely.

"It was fine," Audrey responded. "But I get a little queasy on planes."

"My dad . . . er, Dad could get you some Dramamine," I advised, but she'd already turned her attention back to Mom.

"By the way, Anne, thanks so much for having our seats upgraded!" Audrey said. "Neither of us have ever traveled first class before, and riding in the front of the plane made me less nauseous, I think."

"You're welcome, honey," smiled Mom. "I just wanted you guys to have a good trip. We're so glad you both could come!"

She reached out to squeeze Audrey's arm and they grinned at each other like best girlfriends. A sudden queasiness crept into my stomach that had nothing to do with flying.

Julian came in from behind them; he'd been talking to Dad and Will, who'd stayed outdoors so Dad could have a smoke. That was fine by me; one introduction at a time was all I could handle.

"H-hi," Julian said shyly, and Mom spun around.

"Oh my goodness, Julian!" she laughed happily. "Look who's here! Honey, I'd like you to meet Audrey."

"Hi, Julian," Audrey responded. She didn't hug Julian, but rather reached out to touch his shoulder briefly. I wondered how she knew that he wouldn't feel comfortable being hugged.

"Where's Jake?" asked Mom, looking around. "I was hoping you'd all be here when we got home."

"He's down by the water," Julian volunteered. "I'll go find him." He dashed across the room and out onto the patio, disappearing down the sloping descent to the beach.

"Well," said Mom once again. "If David and Will ever bring the bags inside, you can get unpacked and relax a little. Would you like a cold drink?"

"That would be great," Audrey nodded. "Do you have any—"

"—Diet Coke?" I finished.

She looked at me and grinned. "Exactly what I was hoping for."

"Hang on, I'll get it." I couldn't look at Mom, but out of the corner of my eye I could see her beaming.

When I returned with Audrey's Diet Coke, Dad was

lugging a big suitcase through the door. "Good grief, Audrey, this suitcase weighs a ton. What did you do, bring all your grad school books?"

Audrey laughed out loud, and the tiny hairs on the back of my neck stood up; her throaty laugh sounded exactly like my mom's. My parents appeared not to notice, however, and it occurred to me that they'd probably heard it before.

Audrey reached up to redo her ponytail, and in the split second her hair was around her shoulders I saw that it was longer and darker than it had appeared in the picture. She was pretty, I realized, and seemed so friendly.

"What's Will up to out there?" she asked Dad. "I want him to come in and meet Josey." She smiled at me warmly and it wasn't hard to smile back. Still, I'd imagined this moment for so long that the situation felt kind of unreal, like it was happening on a television show I'd already seen the previews for.

"He's looking for his passport," Dad informed her. "It must have fallen out of his pocket on the ride back, because I know he had it when he came through customs."

Just then, Will appeared in the doorway.

"Found it!" he exclaimed, looking relieved. Will was tall and thinner than he'd looked in his picture, but something else about him seemed different than I remembered.

Audrey reached out and took his hand, drawing him closer to her. "Sweetie," she said. "This is Josey."

"Hey, Josey," Will greeted me casually with a friendly

wave. "It's nice to meet you." Suddenly it hit me; he'd shaved off his goatee.

Will looked around the room. "Wow, this place is amazing!"

"I'm really glad you like it," my mom responded happily. "I was worried that it was almost too big."

"Oh no," Audrey enthused. "It's absolutely beautiful."

She fanned her face with her hand. "I can't believe how hot it is here!" she said. "When we left North Dakota it was below freezing with the wind chill!"

Will nodded. "It was a shock to feel the heat when we got off the plane here."

The conversation continued pleasantly, but I couldn't participate. I was in a state of shock myself, because it had finally and suddenly occurred to me why Will had looked vaguely familiar in that first photograph. With his beard gone, I knew Sarah and Britt would agree with me: in spite of the fact that he was a few years older, my sister's future husband was a dead ringer for Brandon Burke.

15

"Ugh, I don't think I've ever been this full before," groaned Audrey, pushing her plate away. We'd spent the afternoon lounging around the pool, then decided to give Marisol the night off and try one of the local restaurants. She'd recommended Lorenzillo's, a seafood place perched right on the dock overlooking the twinkling Gulf of Mexico. We'd arrived early evening and found a good table under the thatched palalpa, then stuffed ourselves with fresh clams and lobster.

I crumpled up my napkin and leaned back in my chair. The dusk breeze off the water was refreshingly cool against my sunburned face.

Jake was quizzing Audrey. "So," he said, leaning forward. "What was your first thought when you heard that your parents got married and had more kids?"

Audrey looked taken aback. "Well," she said carefully. "I guess I'd say I was taken by complete surprise. I'm probably still adjusting to the idea."

Jake looked pleased. He took a sip of his Dos Equis; since he was almost eighteen, Mom and Dad had allowed him to have a beer with dinner.

"Yeah," he agreed. "We were surprised about you, too."

Audrey nodded. "I'm sure you were," she said. I noticed that she looked a little tired. An afternoon in the Mayan sun can wear a person out, especially if you're not used to it.

She turned to me, seeming to want to change the subject. "Josey, Anne tells me that you're interested in psychology."

"Yes." I nodded, feeling an uneasy lurch in the pit of my stomach. I hoped I hadn't eaten any bad lobster.

"I was around your age when I decided I wanted to be a psychologist, too," Audrey smiled. "Getting there takes a lot of hard work and dedication, but it's a really interesting field, and there are so many directions you can go with it. I'll be happy to help you out any way I can."

Maybe it was because *I* was tired and uncomfortably full, or maybe it was because I'd seen Mom slip an arm around Audrey's waist in a quick hug as they walked into the restaurant, but for some reason I just couldn't accept her generous offer gracefully.

"Actually, I'm thinking of going to medical school," I responded casually, surprising even myself. Deep inside, I knew why I'd said it; sitting by the pool that afternoon, I'd overheard Audrey confide to my mother that sometimes she wished she'd gone to medical school instead of graduate school. Now the words popped out before I could think to stop them.

Audrey raised her eyebrows. "Oh!" she exclaimed, a funny look crossing her face. "I didn't know you were considering medical school," she added quietly.

I'd clearly struck a nerve, and an evil little part of me felt pleased.

"What's this?" my dad asked from farther down table, where he and Will were comparing the attributes of Mexican and American beers. "Did I hear someone say they wanted to go to medical school?"

"Yeah, I've been thinking about it for awhile," I replied bravely. That was my story and I was sticking to it.

"But honey, I thought you wanted to be a psychologist, like Audrey," Mom said, looking confused.

"Well, I've changed my mind," I said, already starting to feel miserable. "Don't get me wrong; psychology is interesting and all that . . . It's just that, well, I've just been thinking of doing something else!"

"Maybe you could be a psychiatrist," suggested Julian. "Then you'd kind of be like both."

Audrey was silent, regarding me with a thoughtful expression. When my eyes met hers she gave me a brief smile that was almost sad, and I quickly looked away.

"All I have to say is, the more doctors in the family, the

better!" exclaimed my dad, raising his own glass of beer in a toast.

He turned to Jake. "How about you, son?" he joked, "Podiatry? Dentistry?"

Jake laughed, before turning to Mom. "Is it okay if I go walk around a little?" he asked. "I'd like to see if I can meet some of the local kids."

"That's fine," she agreed. "Just don't stay out too late; we've got to be at the marina early tomorrow morning."

"Marina?" I inquired, surprised. We never did organized tourist-type activities on our trips. "What have you got planned?"

My mom exhaled a stream of smoke from her after-dinner cigarette. "I was thinking that we could take a day tour to Isla Mujeres tomorrow."

"'The Island of Women,'" translated Jake, looking predictably interested.

"The travel agent said it's just beautiful," my mom continued. "The water around the island is supposed to be amazing; crystal clear and as warm as a bathtub. I asked Marisol and she told me it's only about twenty minutes away by ferry; I figured we can look around for awhile, shop, have lunch, swim, and maybe snorkel . . ."

"I'm in!" exclaimed Julian.

When Mom told him that the island was also a sea turtle sanctuary, the deal was sealed. We finished up dinner, paid the check, and went back to the villa, where we found that Marisol had turned down our bedding and put fresh flowers on each nightstand before leaving for the night.

"Whew, I'm beat," Will said, stretching his long arms over his head. "That sun really took it out of me. How about you, Josey; aren't you tired?"

"Mm-hmm, kind of," I replied, not looking at him directly. Even after half a day, his resemblance to Brandon Burke still unnerved me. It was like having a version of BB himself along on a family trip.

"I think we should all turn in early," Mom said. "The ferry leaves at 9 a.m. sharp."

She was digging through her purse, looking for a lighter, I knew. My parents always have a last cigarette before bed, and Dad was already waiting for her on the veranda.

"I guess I'll wait up for Jake," I told her. My mind was so busy that I knew I wouldn't be able to fall asleep easily, and I wasn't looking forward to spending hours tossing and turning sweatily in my bed.

"Oh, Josey, I was going to do that," my mom assured me. "You should get some rest."

I shrugged. "I don't mind," I said truthfully. "I'm too full to sleep yet anyway."

"Well, alright then." Mom looked uncertain. "Are you sure that you don't want me to stay up with you?"

"No, you and Dad go to bed. I'll wake you if I start falling asleep before he gets back."

She considered, finally shrugging in agreement. Will and Audrey had joined Dad on the patio, and I could hear

Julian in the bathroom, brushing his teeth. Mom moved toward me, glancing out at the veranda.

"So," she said in a conspiratorial voice. "What do you think? Isn't she great?"

I smiled and nodded, knowing that's what she wanted me to do. "Mm-hm."

Mom's eyes were shining. "I'm just so happy that we could do this; have everyone together. You'll never know how much it means to me."

"I know, Mom," I nodded. "It's just that . . . sometimes it feels so weird, you know? I mean, Audrey's supposed to be part of our family, and yet we don't really know her *at all.*"

Mom's look was determined. "That's why this trip is so important," she stressed. "Because it's a *beginning.* It's unfortunate that we are just beginning to know our own child at age twenty-five, and you, your sister, but that's the reality of the situation, and we have to just be grateful that we've been given the opportunity at all."

She reached out to stroke my hair. "Josey," she said, her eyes suddenly growing misty, "I can't wait until you really get to know her better. I just know you and Audrey are going to be so important in each other's lives. It's just such a blessing to me!"

Mom clasped her hands together, and I, seeing the hopeful look on her face, vowed in my heart to try harder.

16

As it turned out, I ended up falling asleep on the couch and missed Jake's return. I awoke the next morning to the sound of Marisol letting herself in, and realized that I had spent the entire night with my head jammed into a corner of the sofa. Consequently, I had a crick in my neck, so I went to sit on the veranda, where another beautiful day was dawning, to try and loosen it up.

As I carefully rotated my head back and forth, I thought about how I seemed to be the only one truly struggling with Audrey's arrival in our family. My parents were clearly crazy about her, and even Julian had taken to gazing at her admiringly by the end of the first day. I had to admit that she was fun to be around, and always had an amusing story to tell or a witty remark to interject. Plus, she was obviously a nice person, someone who I would've probably enjoyed meeting under other circumstances. I knew that even Sarah and Britt would think she was wonderful.

So what is it? I asked myself. Why couldn't I shake the heavy, sick feeling that I'd had in the pit of my stomach ever since that fateful conversation at the kitchen table weeks earlier? Was there something wrong with me?

"Morning, Josey." Audrey herself had come out on the veranda and finished her greeting with a yawn.

"Oh, uh, good morning. How did you sleep?" I asked, startled by her sudden appearance.

"Like a rock," she grinned, then squinted at me. "How about you?"

"Fell asleep on the couch," I admitted. Now she was squinting out over the horizon to where the sun was just cresting.

"Can't you see?" I asked her rudely.

Audrey looked startled, then chuckled. "No, actually, I forgot to bring my glasses and I just woke up so I haven't put my contacts in yet. I can see, but not very well."

"I have contacts too," I admitted. "I've worn glasses since the fifth grade."

Audrey made a face, "Count yourself lucky," she said. "I had to get them in the *first* grade!"

"Wow." I considered that. "Your eyes must be really bad!"

"Yeah, they've been bad as long as I can remember. I really hated wearing glasses when I was a kid, too; they were always sliding down on my nose and my mom was constantly telling me to clean them."

I chuckled. "I know what you mean," I told her honestly. For the short time before I'd gotten contact lenses, my dad would often snatch my glasses off my face to wipe them on his shirt. "I don't know how you can even see through these things," he'd say.

"When I was fourteen my parents finally let me get contact lenses; boy was I happy!" Audrey smiled, remembering. "But because of the shape of my eyes, I had to get hard lenses. They were really uncomfortable at first, but I was absolutely determined to wear them. I remember sitting on the couch watching television with water just *streaming* out of my eyes!"

I turned to look at Audrey's pretty, clear eyes, imagining how they must have been red and irritated as they tried in vain to blink out the hard plastic lenses. Without any makeup on, it was even more apparent why everyone thought we looked alike.

"What are you ladies doing up already?"

It was Dad, coming out for his morning cigarette.

"Good morning!" Audrey reached over to give him a quick hug, bringing a surprised smile to Dad's face.

She didn't seem to notice. "Isn't it beautiful out here?"

"Yes, it certainly is." Dad smiled down at her, and I knew he wasn't talking about the day.

You decided you're going to try harder, remember? I told

myself, and, with that in mind, I said cheerily, "Well, I think I'll go see what Marisol is making for breakfast."

"Gosh, I'm still full from last night!" Audrey moaned. "Unless, of course, she happens to be making French toast . . ."

"Uh, we're in *Mexico*, not France," I reminded her, in what I hoped was a joking tone.

It must have come off alright, because she winked at me and said, "So I guess I shouldn't expect English muffins either?"

After breakfast was finished and Marisol was elbow-deep in soapy dishwater, we packed up our things and headed for the marina. Jake looked like he'd been up all night, and I couldn't resist rubbing it in a little.

"So, the natives worked you over a little," I teased, expecting a sarcastic retort. Surprisingly, I didn't get one.

"Actually, I met some really cool guys," Jake said seriously. "We hung out at this cool club called Coco Bongo for awhile, and then went to Carlos 'n Charlie's. It was a blast!"

"I'm glad you had fun," said Mom. "What time did you finally get back?"

Jake looked sheepish. "Um, to be honest, I probably got about two hours of sleep."

"Jake Muller!"

"I know, I know," he shrugged good-naturedly. "Hey, I'm *here*, aren't I?"

Mom shook her head and was about to answer, but

we'd arrived at Puerto Juarez, where the ferry was docked. Thirty or forty people were milling around the dock area and I could see that some were already on the boat, choosing their seats. Even though it was still early, the sun was beginning to beat down fiercely, and I was glad I'd thought to wear my swimming suit under my clothes.

The whistle blew, signaling everyone to proceed up the ramp. Mom showed our tickets and a man dressed as a pirate motioned us aboard. He had both a scary-looking dagger and some sort of enormous pistol strapped to his waist; a live parrot was perched on his shoulder.

"Recepción a bordo, señorita bonita!" he greeted to me, winking slyly. I hoped he wasn't going to give me any trouble.

The ride to Isla Mujeres was smooth; the sun sparkled and glistened off the water, and the chatter amongst the passengers was a chaos of different languages. Besides Mexican, Japanese, and American tourists, there was a large contingent of scantily clad Brazilians aboard, which kept Jake interested. Julian was captivated by a school of dolphins that raced alongside the slow-moving ferry for several miles, leaping and frolicking in the waves.

"¡Déme todas sus mujeres y su dinero!"

The pirate had appeared out of nowhere to level his pistol menacingly at Dad's head.

"What?" my father laughed, seemingly unconcerned that a stranger wearing an eyepatch was threatening to blow his brains out.

"He's telling you to give him all your money and your women," Jake informed him.

"Well, I don't have any money, so I guess he'd better just take the women," my dad reasoned. He raised his hands in surrender. "Take them," he consented, gesturing toward me, my mom, and Audrey. "They're all yours."

"Boooo!" shouted the Brazilians, who had been watching from across the deck.

Dad chuckled. "Sorry," he called to them apologetically. "My dagger's at the cleaners!"

The pirate lifted the little parrot off of his shoulder and motioned for Mom to hold out her hand. When she did, he transferred the colorful bird from his finger to hers.

"It's not nearly as heavy as it looks!" Mom laughed, and Dad snapped a picture.

The boat docked at Isla Mujeres a short while later, and we disembarked. It was quickly decided that Dad, Will, and the boys would investigate the snorkeling, while Mom, Audrey, and I would check out the shops.

We wandered down the brickstone streets, taking in the faded Caribbean colors of the original clapboard buildings. The relentless sun was hard on paint, it was clear.

"Look at those," pointed Audrey, indicating a display of Mayan masks in a shop window. "They're so beautiful here, but I wouldn't know what to do with them if I brought one home."

"That's how it always is with souvenirs," agreed Mom. "Take seashells, for instance; they seem so beautiful and delicate when you find them on the beach and so dirty and smelly when you unpack them at home."

Audrey laughed appreciatively, and reached out to link her arm through Mom's. They walked on that way, arm in arm, with me lumping along beside them, feeling like a fifth wheel.

"Let's stop in here," Mom proposed as we came to a tiny shop with an array of beautiful silver jewelry displayed in the window.

The cool darkness inside was a welcome relief from the beating sun, although I couldn't see anything at first. Eventually my eyes adjusted, and I saw that the entire place was filled with an assortment of colorful Mayan-themed apparel and cases of jewelry made from silver and semiprecious stones.

"Ooh, let's try some on!" suggested Audrey, leaning over one of the showcases. "Could I see that necklace, the second one from the right?" she asked the shop clerk, who was standing by helpfully.

He slid the door behind the case open and reached in to retrieve it for her. It was a pretty silver chain with a pendant made of coral, but when she looked at herself in the mirror, Audrey started laughing.

"I think I'm a little too sunburned for coral!" she said, turning so we could see that indeed, the orangish stone almost matched the red blooming on her chest.

"How about that one?" suggested Mom. The clerk

obligingly lifted out a delicate bracelet made of silver and lapis from another case and placed it in Mom's hand.

"Oh, that's really pretty," breathed Audrey, and I nodded in agreement. I don't usually wear much jewelry, but I had to admit that the contrast of the deep blue lapis and the bright silver was striking.

"Do you have another one like this?" Mom asked the clerk. She held up the bracelet so that the silver flashed in the sunlight from the window. "I'd like to get one for each of my daughters."

As soon as she spoke the last words, a funny whirring feeling started up in my head, muffling Audrey's delighted response. "Oh Anne, that's so sweet!" she exclaimed.

"Yeah . . . thanks, Mom," I echoed faintly. Oddly, the words sounded unfamiliar to my ears, as if they hadn't come out of my mouth at all. In fact, everything around me suddenly felt a little unreal, like I was part of it but not really part of it. After Mom paid for the bracelets, I followed her and Audrey out, wearing my new bracelet but lagging a few feet behind the other two. I didn't know if it was the heat or what, but on top of the humming in my head, I was also a little dizzy. The sound of Mom and Audrey's cheerful voices drifting back to me like buzzing mosquitos made me nauseated.

"So what do you think, Josette?" Mom said, turning around to look at me. "Should we go on up the street or turn back the other way?"

She stopped mid-sentence, a startled look on her face.

"Josey? Are you alright?"

Mom retraced her steps back to where I had stopped to lean against a doorway, and took my arm.

"You look pale, honey; are you feeling sick?"

"I-I think I just need something to drink," I managed, before I fell abruptly to the sidewalk in a dead faint.

17

Later that afternoon, after my parents were reasonably assured that I was going to survive, we visited the Turtle Sanctuary. To my embarrassment, my dad insisted on renting a golf cart so that I could ride rather than walk to the sanctuary, and no one would listen when I argued. "But I don't feel sick," I protested. "I think the heat just got to me." Inside my own miserable head, however, I knew that we'd been inside an air-conditioned shop when I started to feel funny, and that it had all began the moment that Mom referred to Audrey and me in one breath as "her daughters." No one would need a degree in psychology to figure that one out. I hoped I wasn't going to start passing out whenever anyone referred to Audrey as a member of the family, like some kind of post-hypnotic suggestion.

It turned out that the Isla Mujeres Turtle Sanctuary

was interesting; there was an aquarium with species on display from around the world, and an enclosure with hundreds of young baby turtles that would someday be released back into the wild. Outside of the aquarium, several large saltwater pens held some of the biggest and oldest turtles in the world. A wandering guide told us that some of the turtles were over 100 years old, and many would grow as big as six to eight feet across.

"That's almost as tall as you are, Will!" exclaimed Julian, causing Will to chuckle.

Audrey tousled Julian's hair affectionately. "You're so funny, Julian," she said, making Julian beam.

I leaned over the edge of one of the pens, watching two giant turtles swimming just below the surface. "I wonder what they think about," I mused out loud.

"Probably not much," responded Will. He'd appeared right beside me, making me jump. "Turtles are basically dinosaurs that made it into modern times. For creatures this prehistoric, eating and mating are about the only things on anyone's minds."

"Are you talking about yourself again, honey?" joked Audrey, coming up behind Will.

She draped an arm over his shoulders and peered down into the tank. Giant turtles cruised lazily below.

"The guide was telling me that turtles are very solitary creatures," she said. "In fact, they don't even stay around to take care of their eggs once they lay them; they just go back into the sea and leave them on the beach. When they hatch, the babies have to find their way out of the nest and all the way across the sand to the water by themselves. A lot of them never make it. Isn't that sad?"

I glanced back to see Mom standing behind Audrey, a stricken look on her face.

Our eyes met and I suddenly realized exactly what she was thinking.

Before I could do or say anything to make her feel better, Dad and Julian appeared. They had gone to check out the gift shop and Julian proudly showed me a necklace that he had purchased there. The pendant was a turtle made of silver and inlaid with turquoise.

"Neat," I told him distractedly, feeling worried about Mom. But when I looked for her a moment later she was talking animatedly to Audrey, Will, and Jake about a turtle's sense of smell. I wondered whether I had mistaken the look on her face.

The ferry departed for the mainland at 5 p.m. sharp, so we took a last walk down the cobblestone streets.

"Everybody hop up on that stone wall," my dad instructed. "I want to get a picture."

I was sweaty and dusty, and the last thing I felt like doing was having my picture taken, but I dutifully climbed up to perch between Julian and Audrey.

"Say '*queso*,'" Dad instructed, and we all complied. As he snapped the picture, we heard the horn from the ferry signaling ten minutes until departure, so we wrapped it up and hurried back to the boat.

On the ride to the mainland, the atmosphere on board turned rowdy. Crewmembers cranked up the music and several passengers formed a conga line to dance to "Tequila."

Our group, however, was quiet. Audrey and Will had found a spot near the stern where they had their heads together, talking softly, while Mom sat looking out over the water, her expression contemplative. Jake had taken Julian with him to visit the Brazilians, and Dad wandered around, snapping pictures of us when we weren't looking.

I leaned over to rest my arms on the ship's railing, watching Isla Mujeres fade in the distance. Fingering my bracelet, I rolled the cool silver and lapis beads between my fingers.

Suddenly I felt my mom's hand on my shoulder.

"You feeling better now, sweetie?" she asked me. "Tequila" had finally wound down, so I could hear her.

"Mm-hmm," I nodded.

"Good." With a look of satisfaction, she reached into her shoulder bag for her cigarettes. She leaned back against the rail and lit up. "Boy, I'm beat!" she said, exhaling a stream of smoke. "And hot."

"Yeah, me too," I agreed. "I'm hitting the pool the minute we get back."

Mom nodded in agreement. She was quiet for a few minutes, smoking and thinking. I glanced over at Audrey and Will; Will was rubbing Audrey's back tenderly as she watched something off in the distance.

"Tomorrow's our last day here; can you believe it?" Mom said, looking out over the horizon where the sun was starting to sink. "I don't want it to end."

"Yeah, it's been quite a trip," I allowed.

Mom sighed. "Hopefully only the first of many." She stubbed out her cigarette on the side of the bench, then wiped away the smudge with her fingertip.

"Mm-hmm," I replied. While I was watching them without appearing to, Audrey had turned to rest her head against Will's chest, and for a split second I'd seen her face.

It was streaked with tears.

18

We spent most of the next day lying around the pool. Audrey had gotten too much sun and her forehead was peeling, so she and Mom sat in the shade under an umbrella, working on crossword puzzles. Julian and I were in the pool, choreographing a synchronized swimming routine, while Dad hung out with Will in the Jacuzzi, drinking Coronas. Earlier, Jake had asked permission to go hang out with his new friends from Coco Bongo.

"Fine," said Dad. "But please be back by dinnertime. It's our last night here and it's important to your mother and me that we all spend it together."

Jake agreed and left.

"Point your toes when you're going under," Julian instructed me now. "Then count to three and come up with your arms like this."

He demonstrated the position, holding one arm straight up and the other one out to the side.

"Okay." We practiced it several times until he felt we'd gotten it right.

Mom got out of her pool chair and came over to where we were working on our routine.

"Let's see the whole thing," she said, raising her camera to capture it. We obliged her with a dress rehearsal while Mom snapped pictures, and when we were finished everyone clapped.

Audrey came over and sat on the edge of the pool next to Mom.

"I hate having to spend our entire last day in the shade!" she mourned. "It won't hurt if I just put my legs in the water for awhile."

"I'm going to go and get some more drinks," Mom told her. "Why don't I bring back a hat for you?"

"Sure, that would be great."

Mom set the camera on the edge of the pool and walked off down the path toward our villa. Julian and I went back to working on our routine while Audrey slipped into the water for a quick dip before returning to the edge of the pool.

A few minutes later Dad climbed out of the whirlpool and came over to pick up the camera. "Josey," he called. "Jump up here next to Audrey for a minute. I want to get a picture of you two together."

I swam to the side of the pool and pulled myself up,

dripping. Audrey peered around from behind me and Dad snapped the picture, then had us hold still for a second one.

"Thanks, girls." He smiled. "I'll bet that's going to be my favorite picture of the whole trip."

Mom came back with a tray of sodas and a hat for Audrey. They sat on the edge of the pool together, drinking Diet Coke and talking.

"It's going to be crazy when I get to Minneapolis," I heard Audrey saying. "There will be so much to do, what with trying to unpack, set up my apartment, and start my internship the Monday after I get there."

"So you basically have to get entirely moved in and unpacked in a weekend?" Mom asked, sounding concerned.

"Pretty much. And just before we left Will found out that he has a major project at work that week, so he won't even be able to come along and help me get moved in."

"Oh, Audrey, that's too bad," Mom sympathized. "Can't any of your friends go along and help?"

Audrey shook her head. "They're leaving for their own internships in other states," she explained. "We all start working at the same time."

"I see," Mom said. She was quiet for a moment, thinking.

"You know what?" she said, finally. "With my flight benefits, I can fly from Chicago to Minneapolis for pennies. Why don't I just hop over that weekend and help you get settled?"

In the pool, I froze right in the middle of a complicated series of arm movements. As I've said before, it was highly unusual for Mom to take time off of work, and she'd already done it for the trips to Grand Forks and Cancun. I thought I must've heard wrong; she couldn't possibly be proposing to take *more* time off.

But Audrey was saying how wonderful it was for Mom to offer to help, and Mom was telling Audrey that she had *months* of vacation time saved up and it would be no problem at all. And I was thinking of all the times that Mom worked on Thanksgiving Day and Christmas Eve because she absolutely couldn't take time off of work. In fact, about the only time she *could* miss work was for big family trips planned months in advance. But now, here she was, committing to taking time off a week from now to go spend it with Audrey in Minneapolis. And I knew in my heart that this wouldn't be the last time, either.

At dinner time, my parents chose a restaurant downtown. A taxi took us to Maria Bonitas, where we were greeted by colorful tilework, paintings by local artists, and a lovely glass-enclosed patio with a view of the water.

"I'll have the almond chicken *mole,*" Dad told the waiter, when he came to take our order, "And a *cerveza, por favor.*"

"*Tendré una hamburguesa y papases fritas,*" Julian ordered when it was his turn.

"A hamburger and French fries?" mocked Jake. "We're in Mexico, loser."

Julian made a face. *"Besa mi nalgas,"* he muttered under his breath, but loud enough for Jake to hear. Jake's mouth fell open.

"What did he say?" my dad asked, looking back and forth between us.

"Um, he said Jake could give him a big kiss," I translated, censoring.

Jake's face was red; he wasn't used to being insulted in his precious Spanish.

"Estas un burro feo," he whispered to Julian, who looked pleased that Jake had considered him worthy of returning an insult.

"Really?" mused Julian, obviously up to the game. He thought for a moment, then brightened.

"Caballo que apesta," Julian suggested, smiling at Jake endearingly.

Jake looked impressed. Clearly he'd underestimated his younger brother up until this point. "What are they teaching him in that Spanish class, anyway?" he demanded to know.

I turned to Audrey and Will, who were looking as lost as my parents. "So, when are you two planning to get married?" I asked.

"Actually, we haven't really decided," Audrey said. "I'll be gone for a year on my internship, and then we'll have to see where I can find a job."

"And we're crossing our fingers that I'll be able to find something in the same area," Will added.

Audrey smiled. "You'll have no problem," she assured

him. Turning back to me, she explained, "Electrical engineers are hard to find. Will should be able to get a job anywhere we go."

"That's good," I responded, not knowing what else to say. Beside me, Jake was hissing Spanish obscenities across the table at Julian, who was giggling uncontrollably.

"Of course, we'd love to stay in Grand Forks," Audrey continued. "Will works for a great firm, and I think they'd be smart to keep him."

I nodded. All those hours performing water ballet had worn me clean out, and I suddenly barely had the strength to make conversation.

My parents had finished ordering and were sitting quietly at the head of the table, smoking and watching the rest of us. Dad's expression was happy and relaxed; his eyes behind the wafting cigarette smoke looked droopy, and I could see that he was feeling almost as sleepy as I suddenly was. Mom was smiling too, but something in her face was different. I looked closer, and the moment I realized what it was I quickly looked away: her eyes were moist and the tense position of her mouth told me that she was struggling to hold back tears.

19

The next morning it was a mad scramble for us all to eat breakfast and get packed. Audrey and Will's flight left at 10:30 and ours left at 11:45, so it made sense for us to leave for the airport at the same time.

I stuffed my dirty clothes into the plastic bag I'd brought for that purpose and opened my suitcase. At the bottom lay my "nature versus nurture" notebook; I'd brought it along hoping to ask Audrey some questions to complete her profile, but it just had never seemed like the right time to bring it out.

By 9:30, we'd said goodbye to Marisol and were on our way to the airport. I was dreading the long day of travel ahead, but it would be good to sleep in my own bed tonight. Sarah and Britt would be calling, too, wanting to hear all the details of our trip.

"I can't believe it's time to leave already," Audrey mourned as we pulled into the airport parking lot. "Three days just went by so fast." She looked genuinely sad, and my mom reached over the back of the seat to squeeze her hand.

"Don't worry, sweetie pie," she reassured her, calling Audrey by the pet name she generally reserves for Julian. "We'll start planning right away for our next family get-together. In fact, we can talk about it next weekend, when I come to Minneapolis."

Audrey smiled at her wanly. Will was sitting between us in the middle seat, quiet as usual, and I felt him pull away from me slightly as he gave Audrey a squeeze.

"I'll drop you all off at Audrey and Will's gate, then go and return the rental car," my dad said, pulling up to the curb.

"Just make sure you get back to the gate before they have to board," my mom reminded him worriedly. She'd burned through three cigarettes during the drive, so I knew she was feeling on edge.

"I'll do my best," Dad promised. I knew he'd try to hurry, but it's always hard to know how quickly or slowly things are going to happen when you're in another country.

We all piled out of the Suburban and loaded up with our stuff. Fortunately, the lines inside the terminal weren't long, so we were able to check our bags and make it to the holding area in good time.

"Man, traveling sucks," Jake complained, dropping

into an uncomfortable plastic airport chair. Predictably, he was depressed about having to leave Mexico.

"Yeah," Audrey agreed. "But it's always good to get home." She'd grown quieter after Dad dropped us off.

"Do you have the tickets?" she asked Will for the third time. Will nodded, smiling at her patiently. He caught my eye and gave me a wink.

We sat in silence, watching the flow of travelers. People-watching in airports is always interesting, no matter where you are.

"I'm sorry," my mom said apologetically, standing up and grabbing her purse. "I've just got to run outside for one last cigarette."

I knew then that she must be really uptight; she usually can at least make it through the first flight back to the States before she cracks. "I promise I'll be quick."

She looked at me. "Josey, could you have me paged if they call Will and Audrey's flight?"

I nodded "sure" and Mom took off. Julian was immersed in his Game Boy and Jake was listening to music on his headphones, so that left me, Audrey, and Will sitting there.

"Um, so how did you guys meet?" I asked, in the interest of making conversation.

They both chuckled. "Well," said Audrey. "I had a work-study job at the campus bowling alley, and Will came in there with some of his friends."

"And your eyes met while you were spraying out his bowling shoes?" I finished, joking.

Audrey grinned. "Something like that." She squeezed Will's hand, and he smiled down at her with clear affection.

"Actually," she said. "He just came up and started talking to me. And, well, I guess the rest is history."

"Really?" I asked. It was hard to picture quiet Will initiating a conversation with a pretty counter girl, even in a bowling alley.

"You look surprised," Audrey smiled.

"Yeah, well," I said. "It's just hard to picture Will hitting on you. I mean, he's so quiet. Not like you," I blathered on thoughtlessly. "You're . . . well, you talk ALL-L-L-L THE T-I-I-I-I-ME!"

Of course, I didn't *really* drag the words out endlessly, but in the space between me and Audrey the words "all the time" seemed to stretch out and hang in the air like a stringy black cloud. I watched helplessly as the happy expression seemed to melt from Audrey's face in slow motion, to be replaced by a crushed, dispirited look that told me I'd unintentionally insulted her terribly.

Unfortunately, my mind chose that moment to freeze up so completely that I simply sat there and stared at her, a silly half-grin still pasted to my face as I cast around in my head for some way to rectify the situation. I knew I'd somehow hurt Audrey's feelings, and I saw tears spring to her eyes before she turned quickly away.

"I made it!" Dad announced, appearing behind us. He glanced around. "Where's Mom?"

"Here she comes," pointed Jake, taking off his headphones. We looked and saw Mom sprinting down the concourse. Or at least sprinting as much as a heavy smoker can sprint.

"Did they call your flight yet?" she panted to Audrey, who shook her head wordlessly. Mom took one look at her face, and stopped short. "Honey, are you alright?"

Audrey nodded, and from where I sat next to her I could see the effort it took for her to paste on a smile and nod to reassure my mom. "Fine," she managed. "I'm fine."

Just then they *did* call for Audrey and Will's flight to begin boarding, and we all got to our feet to begin the awkward process of saying goodbye.

"You take care of yourself, sweetie," said my dad, hugging Audrey long and hard.

"Thanks for everything," I heard her say in a voice muffled by Dad's shoulder.

Mom was hugging Will. "We'll see you soon," she promised. She held her arms out to Audrey. "And I'll see *you* next week!"

"I'm looking forward to it," Audrey murmured, hugging her back.

She turned toward me. "Josey?" she said, not meeting my eyes. "It was good to meet you. Take care."

I nodded, feeling terrible as she leaned in to give me a hug. I knew I should apologize for my careless words, but there wasn't time and I couldn't think of what I might say.

We finished up our goodbyes and stood around watching as Audrey and Will had their tickets checked by the gate agent before boarding the plane. Audrey glanced back for a final wave, her face unreadable, and then they were gone.

Mom heaved a big sigh. "It's so hard to see them go," she said. "I just hope this was a good experience for her."

Dad put an arm around her shoulders. "I think it was," he assured her. "And don't worry; like you said, you'll see her in a few days."

Mom nodded. She turned to me anxiously, "How about you, Josey; do you think things went okay?"

"Mm-hm," I nodded. Inside I felt uneasy, but there was no way to explain to my parents that I'd unintentionally said something mean to Audrey just before she'd left.

Mom continued. "Do you feel like you got a chance to get to know Audrey, at least a little?" Her earnest look told me the answer she needed to hear.

"Of course," I nodded. "Audrey's nice. And it feels more and more like, well, like she's part of the family."

I looked down at my daughter bracelet, twisting it guiltily between my fingers. I must have pulled too hard, because suddenly it broke, the silver and blue beads spilling loosely into my hand.

"Oh no!" I exclaimed, trying to make sure none escaped. "My bracelet broke!"

Mom helped me gather the beads, then examined the

broken string. "We can have this fixed when we get home," she observed. "It looks like the string just snapped."

"I think I might have accidentally pulled on it," I admitted, feeling guilty.

"Don't feel bad, sweetie," Mom soothed. "It's nothing that can't be fixed."

I sure hope you're right, I thought miserably.

20

"I still can't believe how much he looks like Brandon Burke!" breathed Britt, examining a picture of Will for the hundredth time. It seemed like that was all she'd done since I'd gotten back from Cancun.

I nodded. To tell the truth, meeting Will and Audrey had kind of ruined the whole BB thing for me. Now whenever I looked at Brandon Burke I saw my sister's fiancé, which made me feel uneasily like I was lusting after my own brother-in-law.

It was the weekend after I'd gotten back, and Britt, Sarah, and I were at my house studying for our second-to-last psychology test. Mom had made sure that we were stocked up with necessary supplies before she left for Minneapolis; Doritos crumbs were scattered across the floor of my bedroom and we were already deep into the M&Ms.

"We'd better get back to studying, Britt," cautioned Sarah. "You know you've got to do well on this exam."

Britt tossed the picture of Will aside. "I know," she whined. "But today's Saturday; I just don't *feel* like studying! Why can't we go to the mall for a little while?"

Sarah shrugged. "I'm not your mother," she told Britt. "Go ahead and go to the mall if you want. But don't blame us if you get a bad grade on the test."

Britt made a face. "Alright," she said petulantly. "But don't forget that we still have to get Josey a dress."

Preparations for the Holidazzle dance were in full swing. Johnny Hudson had screwed up the courage to ask Britt while I was in Mexico, and I'd resigned myself to the idea that I'd be spending the night of Hollidazzle at home in front of the television.

"I *told* you that I'm not going," I reminded her. "I'm not going to tag along with you guys like a fifth wheel."

While I'd been away in Mexico, Sarah had developed cold feet about going to the dance with someone other than me and Britt. "Oh come on," she pleaded, forgetting about the psychology test herself for a moment. "It wouldn't be like that!"

"Besides," she added. "There are still a few weeks left before the dance . . . maybe someone will ask you. Then we could all go together."

I made a sour face. "I'm not holding my breath," I told her.

"Who's BB going with again?" Britt asked, picking up the picture of Will for the hundred-and-first time.

"Mallory Larson," I reminded her. "Varsity cheerleader. Popular. Gorgeous. You get the picture."

"Oh, yeah." We were all silent for a moment, thinking our separate thoughts. I took a swig of my Diet Coke, feeling the tiny bubbles float up to tickle my nose.

"How are you coming with your 'nature versus nurture' project?" asked Sarah out of the blue, interrupting my reverie.

I hedged. "Oh, fine," I told her. The truth was, I hadn't worked on it at all since our trip to Cancun. Every time it came into my mind I quickly pushed the thought away. I knew I'd have to do something soon, however; the paper was due at the end of the Fall/Winter semester, which was quickly approaching. First there was Monday's test, followed closely by Thanksgiving, the Holidazzle dance, finals, and finally Christmas break. Life seemed to have suddenly picked up speed.

Dad stuck his head in the door. "Josey, it looks like I have to run over to the pharmacy," he told me. "Mike called and they're swamped. Can you hold down the fort here so I can go lend a hand?"

I shrugged. "Sure." Jake was at work and I knew that Julian was out in the driveway with Ross, fooling around on their bikes. November in Woodridge had turned out to be unusually warm, and there wasn't even any snow on the ground yet.

"Thanks," Dad said. "Hopefully I won't be gone for more than a few hours."

"No problem. We've got lots of studying to do." I threw a look at Britt, whose expression was glum.

Dad gave me some instructions about starting dinner, and departed. I heard the back door close as he left.

"Why don't I quiz you two on the personality disorders?" proposed Sarah. Britt sighed and let her head loll dramatically onto her chest.

"There are ten of them . . ." Sarah prompted, ignoring her.

We were up to "histrionic" when I heard the back door bang open. Sarah didn't even glance up from her notebook, but Britt looked at me suddenly and I would later remember that a psychic awareness that something was terribly wrong passed between us.

A split second later, a chilling shriek tore through the air. "Josey! Help! Help! Julian's hurt!"

I scrambled off the bed, out door, and down the stairs, Sarah and Britt at my heels. Ross was standing in the kitchen, trembling. His face was stark white and his T-shirt was stained with fresh blood.

"Oh my God," I gasped, feeling faint. Britt pushed past me.

"Where is he?" she demanded. Ross pointed toward the garage door.

We followed Britt outside and down the driveway to where Julian lay, face down, a pool of blood spreading around him. His bicycle was lying a few feet away, its front wheel still spinning lazily to a stop.

"Julian? Julian?" Britt called urgently, kneeling down beside him. She reached out to touch his limp arm gently.

"Shouldn't we turn him over?" Sarah asked in a strangled voice. "What if he can't breathe?"

Britt shook her head. "We can't move him," she said. "We don't know if he has any broken bones." Hearing that, black spots began to swim before my eyes, and I reached out to Sarah to steady myself.

Julian moaned and began to stir. "M-m-mom?" he murmured. I forced myself forward and knelt down beside him.

"Julian, we're here," I told him. "You've had an accident, and . . . you're hurt pretty bad. Just lie still. We're going to get some help."

"No, I'm okay," Julian responded, rolling over onto his side and trying to sit up. We all gasped; his face was a mess of blood and gravel, and his front teeth were broken into jagged points. "I'm just kind of . . . dizzy. And my head hurts."

He turned and spat blood and bits of teeth onto the cement. "Boy," he said, looking at the pool of blood beside him. "Dad's gonna be mad. We'd better hose the driveway off."

"No, he won't," I assured him.

Britt turned to Sarah. "Look, he's confused," she said. "I think we'd better take him to the emergency room."

Sarah looked doubtful. "He's still bleeding," she pointed out. "Mom will kill me if we get blood in her car. Maybe we should just call Josey's dad and tell him to come home."

"I don't think we can wait," I said, eyeing Julian's face, which was swelling rapidly. "It would take Dad at least twenty minutes to drive back here, and then another twenty minutes to get to the hospital. It'll just be quicker if we call and tell him to meet us at there."

I looked at Julian, who had laid back on the driveway again. "Besides, what if he's got some kind of concussion?"

Sarah considered for a minute. "Alright," she said finally. "But we're going to have to bring a towel or something."

"I'll grab one." Britt jumped up and ran into the house. Ross and I helped Julian get unsteadily to his feet while Sarah moved the bike off of the driveway onto the lawn.

"We'll get him into the car," she said to me when Britt came back with a towel. "Why don't you run in and call your dad?"

"Okay." I darted into the house and dialed the number, leaning against the wall. My legs were shaky, and my heart was pounding. When I got Dad on the line I explained quickly what had happened, and he agreed that the best plan was for him to meet us at the hospital.

"Please tell Sarah to drive carefully," my dad said, sounding understandably rattled. "One accident is enough."

On the way to the hospital, Julian's lip stopped bleeding, but he continued to babble on about seemingly unrelated topics like his teacher and the time he'd taken the train to visit our cousins in Michigan. Watching him worriedly, I suddenly noticed a few drops of bright red blood inside his ear.

"Please hurry," I called to Sarah, trying not to let the fear show through my voice.

"I'm doing the best I can," she said, her eyes fixed determinedly on the road. I didn't know if I should encourage her to break the speed limit or not, but I didn't want to distract her. Ross kept turning around to throw anxious glances back at us from the front seat, while Britt sat stroking Julian's arm and murmuring to him softly after he stopped talking and sank into a kind of foggy silence that scared me even more than his nonsensical babbling had.

Finally we reached the hospital and Sarah pulled up in front of the emergency entrance. "Whew," she said, giving a big sigh. "I never want to drive an ambulance!"

Britt had jumped out of the car and run into the hospital the minute the car had stopped. Now she was back, followed by an orderly pushing a wheelchair.

"Let's get him inside quickly," the orderly instructed. "Is he able to get out of the car?"

"He's confused and disoriented," Britt said expertly, and we all nodded. I was impressed by how unruffled Britt had remained throughout the entire ordeal. She'd taken charge and didn't seem to be a bit flustered, even when a glossy bubble of blood had swelled from one of Julian's nostrils, causing Ross to exclaim, "Eww, dude!"

Now Julian was muttering incoherently again, but his eyes were open and he was able to get out of the back seat and into the wheelchair with the orderly's support. "Has anyone notified his family?" the orderly asked, swinging the chair around to propel it through the entrance.

"I-I'm his sister," I spoke up. "I've called my dad. He should be here soon."

The orderly nodded. "Then why don't you go ahead and start filling out paperwork with the receptionist? I'll take your brother back to an exam room." He called the last words back over his shoulder as he pushed Julian's chair through the electric doors, which swung open automatically as they approached.

"Come on, Josey," said Sarah, when after I didn't move for a moment. She put an arm around my shoulders. "I'll help you."

We were just finishing giving the receptionist Julian's identifying information when my dad burst through the lobby doors. "Where's Julian?" he demanded, seeing us. "What's his condition?"

"I don't know anything yet," I admitted miserably. "They said the doctor would come out and talk with us when they're finished examining him."

Tears had gathered behind my eyes but I was afraid to let them out. I felt like if I let anyone see how scared I was, it would be like admitting to myself that something *really* serious had happened to Julian.

My dad paced the waiting room until the receptionist asked him to sit down and answer some questions about Julian's insurance, past medical history, and so on. While he was doing that, Sarah and Britt sat with me, each holding one of my hands.

"My mom's going to freak out," I said, wishing like anything that she were here. Mom is always good at remaining calm in crisis situations.

"Julian will be alright," Sarah assured me earnestly. "He will."

Britt was quiet, which made me more nervous than ever.

Just then the door to the examining area swung open and a tall blond woman appeared. "Muller family?" she called, looking around.

"That's us," said Dad, jumping to his feet. The doctor came over to where we were sitting.

"I'm Dr. Gaul," she said, holding out her hand to shake Dad's. She was calm and reassuring in her white jacket.

"I've just examined your son, and he's clearly had a bad concussion. He's become more alert, but as a precaution, I've sent him down to radiology for a CAT scan. We need to make sure that he hasn't had a skull fracture, and that he doesn't have any bleeding in his brain."

I gasped, horrified to think that my little brother may actually have cracked his skull.

Dr. Gaul continued, looking at me now, "As I said, a CAT scan is primarily a precaution. When he gets done there we'll suture the laceration in his lip, and probably get the orthodontist in here to consult. Looks like your brother knocked out a few of his permanent teeth."

She smiled at me, and I suddenly felt a little better. Dr. Gaul seemed confident and unworried; Julian was clearly in good hands.

"Thank you, Doctor," Dad said gratefully. "When can we see him?"

Dr. Gaul looked at her watch. "After radiology finishes with him, maybe in a half hour or so," she figured. "I'd also like to admit him to the hospital overnight, for observation."

"Of course," Dad agreed. "In fact, I'd feel better if you would."

"Fine, then. I'll let the nursing staff know to start the admission paperwork." With that, Dr. Gaul went back through the swinging door, presumably off to her next emergency.

Dad sank back down into the chair. "Good grief," he said. "Who would've thought that something like this would happen while your mother was gone? I'm just thankful that Julian's going to be alright."

I was silent. If Mom hadn't thought it was so important to go and help Audrey move, nothing like this probably would have happened. Mom was always on Julian's case about wearing his bike helmet when he was riding.

And if this *had* happened, Mom would have known how to handle things. She certainly wouldn't have cared about getting a speeding ticket on the way to the hospital.

I suddenly remembered that Mom was the first one Julian had asked for after he'd been hurt. Tears began to build behind my eyes again, but this time they weren't tears of fear or sadness. These were angry tears, hot, bitter, and salty, burning into my brain with anger for Julian's sake, anger for my sake . . . anger for the sake of everything that had changed and would never, ever, be the same again.

21

The CAT scan showed that Julian *did* have a hairline skull fracture, so everyone was glad he would be staying overnight in the hospital. Dr. Gaul assured us that there was no evidence of bleeding in his brain, and the fracture was not likely to cause him any long-term problems.

"He'll just have to be careful for awhile until he's all healed up," she told us. "No skateboarding or biking without a helmet, no wrestling around or contact sports . . ."

"Don't worry," Dad assured her. "I have a feeling that once his mother gets back he's going to be taking it *very* easy."

He had finally gotten a hold of Mom and she was flying home on the next plane out of Minneapolis.

Julian looked terribly small and wan lying in the big hospital bed, his head wrapped in gauze and sutures running through his lip. "Hey," he said, lifting a hand to wave weakly as we filed in. "How'th it goin'?"

The nurse had warned us that she'd given him some pain medication for his headache, so we could expect him to be a little lethargic and confused.

"How's your head feeling, buddy?" Jake asked. Dad had called him at work, and he'd come right over to the hospital.

"Mmm, it kinda hurtth," Julian murmured. Without his front teeth he sounded like a kindergartner. His face was swollen and the area around his eyes was beginning to turn a deep shade of purple, like a raccoon.

"Boy, you must have fallen right on your face," Britt observed. Julian didn't answer; he appeared to have drifted off, but Ross spoke up.

"He pretty much *did* fall right on his face," he explained. "We were trying to do a BMX trick, and Julian lost his grip and went over the handlebars."

I shuddered, picturing the sequence of events. What had ever possessed them to be so reckless? Mom was going to have a cow when she heard what had happened.

Dad was stroking Julian's hair where it was sticking out of the dressing. "Looks like he's going to be out again for awhile," he said. "Why don't you guys go home and I'll sit with him."

He looked at Jake. "Maybe you could bring me back a change of clothes later on," he instructed. "The nurse said that they'll bring in a rollaway so I can spend the night."

I took a deep breath. "Dad, would it be all right if I stayed too?" I asked. "I-I feel sort of responsible for Julian getting hurt. I mean, I was supposed to be in charge of things, and I guess that we just got too involved in our studying, and . . . and then we heard the door slam open and Ross was yelling and . . ."

I trailed off helplessly as my words deteriorated into sobs.

Arms came around me from several directions. I could smell my dad's spicy aftershave, Britt's *Glitter* perfume, and the clean scent of Sarah's shampoo.

"It *wasn't* your fault at all, honey," Dad's voice spoke, close to my ear. "It was a complete and total accident, and the last thing anyone wants is for you to blame yourself."

My body shook with sobs; I tried to speak, but no words came, only more tears.

"Besides," Dad continued gently. "Every boy gets a few stitches along the way. When the story gets around among his friends, he'll be a big celebrity, right, Ross?"

I didn't see Ross's reaction because I couldn't lift my head off my dad's shoulder. I felt Britt's warm hand gently rubbing my back, and Sarah reached out to smooth a piece of hair behind my ear.

"Come on, Josey," she coaxed softly. "He'll be all right. Everything's going to be all right."

Dad insisted that I go home, and I finally went, but my sleep that night was fitful and filled with recurring nightmares of Julian crashing face-first onto the cement driveway. In my dreams I saw that he was going to fall and tried to call out to him, but no words would come out of my mouth, and when I tried to reach him in time the air through which I moved had turned gluey and thick. I awoke the next morning feeling foggy-headed and exhausted.

"Morning, glory," Dad greeted me when I came into the kitchen. He was sitting at the table with coffee and a cigarette, reading the morning paper.

"What? I thought you were going to stay at the hospital," I asked him, alarmed.

He shrugged. "I did stay until around midnight, when your mom got there. She came straight to the hospital after her plane landed. There was only one extra bed available, so I came home."

I sank down into a chair. "Have you talked to Mom today?" I asked. "How's Julian doing?"

"Julian's fine," my dad smiled. "He still has a headache and is a little nauseated, but he managed to eat some toast for breakfast. The doctor should be by to examine him around eleven this morning, and if he's able to give his name, rank, and serial number they'll most likely be discharging him home."

"That's good," I said, leaning on my elbows to rub my tired eyes. I had a headache too. Suddenly it occurred to me to ask, "What about his teeth?"

"The orthodontist stopped by after you left last night. He said that they'll wait for everything to heal up, then decide what to do. I imagine they'll probably fit him with a bridge of some kind."

"A bridge? Like old people wear?"

Dad laughed. "Something like that. He thought he could maybe cap one of the teeth, but the other two were knocked out pretty cleanly."

Seeing my face, he added, "Don't worry, Josey. Julian's probably going to end up thinking this is the coolest thing that ever happened to him."

I reached out to fiddle with the salt shaker. "I just can't help feeling that it should never have happened."

Dad made a face. "Things like this happen all the time, Josette, especially to young boys."

He leaned forward and took the salt shaker from me, replacing it next to the pepper shaker where it belonged. Dad hates it when people fiddle with things.

"How about if I make some French toast?" he suggested. "A good breakfast will make us both feel better."

French toast, I thought, and remembered that it was Audrey's favorite.

"I think I'll just have some juice," I said, avoiding his look of disappointment. "I'm not very hungry."

I spent the rest of the morning lying on my bed, listening to the radio. I knew I should be studying for the next day's psychology test, but in light of everything that had happened it just didn't seem important.

Sarah called around ten thirty. "Have you heard how Julian is this morning?" she asked.

"Yeah, my mom's at the hospital with him." I briefed her on the information my dad had given me.

"Well, that's good news anyway," Sarah said, sounding relieved. "What did your mom say about the whole thing?"

A cold feeling crept into my chest. "I don't know," I answered briefly. "I haven't seen her yet."

Sarah asked whether I wanted to get together with her and Britt to pick up studying for the psychology test, but I told her to go ahead without me.

"I'll catch up with you guys after Julian gets home," I promised. "I won't be able to concentrate until I can see for sure that he's all right."

We hung up and I went back up to my room. The "nature versus nurture" notebook was lying on the floor, and I kicked it underneath the bed as I passed by. Lying down on the rumpled covers felt unbelievably good, and within fifteen minutes I had fallen fast asleep.

Julian and Mom arrived home shortly after lunch. Julian was alert and in good spirits, although he still felt a little unsteady and was moving gingerly.

"Let's get you right into bed," Mom told him. "You heard Dr. Gaul. It's 'minimal activity' for at least a few days."

"Can't I at leath call Roth?" Julian pleaded. "I want him to come over and thee my fathe."

He gave her a pitiful look, which wasn't difficult considering that his face was still pretty swollen and his bruises were an impressive rainbow of colors in the red/purple spectrum.

"Don't worry," Dad told him. "I guarantee you're going to look worse before you look better."

Julian seemed cheered by this idea and allowed himself to be led upstairs to his bedroom, Dad and I trailing behind. Mom set him up in bed with lots of pillows, the television remote, a glass of juice, and a bell to ring if he needed her.

"You're not to get up for *anything*, even to go to the bathroom, without help," she instructed him. I expected Julian to argue, but he merely nodded tiredly and settled back into the pillows. Clearly the trip from the hospital had worn him out.

Mom shut the bedroom door behind us and for the first time turned her attention to me. "Whew!" she said, giving me a weak smile. "What a scary thing to be called home for!"

I knew she expected me to commiserate with her, but I couldn't bring myself to say anything at all. Some part of me, deep inside, still felt dark and angry about the fact that Mom wasn't where she should have been when Julian got hurt. Instead, she was off spending time with Audrey, who seemed much more important to her these days than any of the rest of us.

Oblivious to my bitter thoughts, Mom began prattling on about her trip to Minneapolis: how worried Audrey had been when she'd heard about Julian's accident, how barren Audrey's apartment was, Audrey's friendly new roommate, a restaurant where she and Audrey had eaten . . .

"How can you even *talk* about this?" I exploded suddenly, my feet skidding to a halt. We'd arrived in the kitchen where I could still smell the vanilla and cinnamon from the French toast that Dad had apparently made after all.

Mom froze, turning to blink at me in surprise. "What do you mean?" she asked, genuinely confused.

"Here's what I mean: Julian is lying up there with a terrible concussion and still all you can think about is 'Audrey this, Audrey that' . . . you'd think that she was your only child, for God's sake!" I didn't even try to stop the words as they flew out of my mouth. I felt like I was going to vomit with fury.

"Josey," Mom began. "I-I don't know what to say! I feel awful if you think that . . ."

"Why *wouldn't* I think it?" I demanded. "Ever since Audrey showed up, everything's always about her. You couldn't care *less* about what's going on with the rest of us! The only person who's important to you is Audrey; what she's doing, where she's doing it, who she's doing it with . . . anything, as long as it's about her!"

I paused for breath. In a final burst, I sputtered, "You . . . you even acted like you didn't even know for sure that I wanted to be a psychologist." The last part sounded weak, I knew, but the word came straight from the well of hurt deep within my heart.

Mom was silent for a moment, searching my face with her eyes.

"Oh, sweetie," she said finally, her voice thick with emotion. "I wish I would have known that you felt this way!

I'm so terribly sorry if I've made you feel neglected. I love you and your brothers more than you can imagine; you're the most important people in the world to me . . ."

She reached up to wipe away several anguished tears that had filled her eyes and slipped down her face. "It breaks my *heart* to think that anything I've done has made you question that!"

I looked down at the floor. Mom had never talked to me like this before, never said so openly how much she loved me. It made me feel both good and kind of crummy at the same time.

My throat was aching with weeks of accumulated uncried tears. "Sometimes it just seems like your mind is full of Audrey and there's no room for the rest of us anymore," I told her miserably.

"Oh, Josey," Mom said. I looked up and my green eyes met Mom's warm brown ones. The look in those eyes told me that I had been wrong about everything. Maybe Mom didn't love me in exactly the same way as she loved Audrey, but she certainly loved me just as much.

"I need to know how to fix this," Mom was saying, wiping her wet cheeks. "How can I make things right?"

I sighed, and reached over to the counter for a Kleenex. I handed it to her, then took one for myself.

"I think . . . maybe you just did," I told her.

22

Later that night, my head cleared enough that I realized with a start that I wasn't at all prepared for the next morning's psychology test. I was half-heartedly gathering my notes off the floor, where I'd left them what seemed like ages ago, when my parents knocked softly at the door.

"Josette, can we talk to you?" Mom asked, coming in to sit on the edge of my bed. Dad followed her, perching on the chair beside my desk.

"Sure," I said with resignation. I'd been halfway expecting this.

Mom and Dad looked at each other and I knew they were silently trying to decide who should start. Dad won.

"The thing is, sweetie," Mom said. "Your father and I were talking about how you've kind of been . . . struggling, lately. And that's probably largely our fault."

She sighed. "It's just that you're always so capable and on top of things that sometimes we tend to forget that you're also very sensitive and emotional. If we'd have thought things through better, we would have realized that *of course* you would react strongly to Audrey coming into our lives."

I opened my mouth to object, but Dad cut me off.

"Josey, it was a shock to all of us when Audrey came back into our lives, and for the most part, it's been a wonderful thing for our family." He paused, and looked at me seriously, "In retrospect, however, Mom and I have realized that perhaps we could have handled things better, and certainly that we could have been more aware of how you were feeling. It must have been really upsetting to you to suddenly be told that you have a sister, and to find yourself with some unexpected competition for the role of 'first daughter' in the family."

Having both my parents looking at me so tenderly and sympathetically was too much; big fat tears welled up in my eyes and ran down my face. I nodded, feeling the rest of the tension that had been building inside me over the past six weeks come bubbling to the surface.

"It *has* been upsetting, to be completely honest," I choked out. "It seemed like you both just thought Audrey was so perfect and wonderful, and it made me feel . . . kind of lousy." I cried harder at the shameful words, but at least they were finally the truth.

Mom slid off the bed to sit beside me on the floor. She wrapped her arms around me and hugged me as I cried myself out, Dad dispensing Kleenex from the box on my desk.

Eventually I was able to get a hold of myself, and Mom adjusted her position to see me better. I knew I looked awful; I hadn't even combed my hair since the day before, and crying always makes my whole face get red and puffy.

Mom waited until my hiccupping had stopped before she spoke. "Josey, I have a proposition to make, something that I think might eventually help you feel better about things."

I noticed she had used the word *eventually*, meaning, I guessed, that what she was about to propose wasn't necessarily going to be something I would enjoy. I didn't say anything, waiting to hear her proposal.

"I've been thinking," she began, and then blushed a little nervously. "Or actually, I guess I should say that Audrey and I were *talking* when I was in Minneapolis, even before Julian got hurt." Mom took a deep breath, "Josey, I think that it might be a good idea for you to go to Minneapolis and spend some time alone with Audrey."

I was shaking my head before she even finished.

"I really don't want to," I told her. "Besides, I've got too much to do with school and everything. This just isn't a good time."

Dad spoke up. "I think it's a good idea too, Josey. Maybe if you and Audrey got to know each other a little better and talked things out, some of the feelings that are riding so high right now could be put to rest."

I didn't say anything. The last thing I wanted to do was go and spend time alone with Audrey.

My mom gave me another hug, then released me and got to her feet. "All we ask is that you think about it, sweetie; it really has to be your decision."

She reached down to stroke the top of my head with her fingertips. "You might be surprised to know that this situation has been hard on Audrey too. Maybe you and she have something else in common besides the obvious: you're both going through a difficult experience that few other people could fully understand."

She tapped me on the head, not unkindly, in emphasis, and went to check on Julian. My dad got up to follow, leaning down to drop a kiss on my forehead as he passed. "You've had a big weekend," he said. "Don't stay up too late studying."

After he was gone, I stared at my psychology notes for a few more minutes, then slowly shut the binder. My brain was full, and I knew I wasn't going to be able to absorb any more information tonight. For the first time ever I'd be going into a test poorly prepared, and frankly, I really didn't even care.

The next morning I discovered that I was even less prepared for the psychology test than I had thought.

"Man, that was a killer," moaned Britt, coming out of the psychology room after the test. Even Sarah looked worried.

"I just wish we'd spent more time reviewing the anxiety disorders," she muttered. "And I wish there were more questions on schizophrenia; we had that section down cold."

I walked along beside them, not saying anything. Aside from the stuff that we'd studied before Julian's accident, I wasn't feeling completely confident about any of the answers I'd given on the test. It was a new and unnerving experience to be so uncertain of how I'd done on a test, especially a *psychology* test.

Britt was already tossing any concerns about the test to the wind.

"Three weeks until Hollidazzle!" she sang as we passed by a colorful banner advertising the dance. "Which means just three weeks for us to find you a date!" she reminded me.

"I told you, I'm not going," I informed her, not caring if I sounded crabby. "To tell you the truth, I don't even *want* to go anymore."

"Oh come on." Britt was relentless. "Why wouldn't you want to go?"

I brooded silently. "I may not even be here that weekend," I said finally.

Both Britt and Sarah turned to look at me. "Not be here for the Hollidazzle?" Sarah said, "Where are you going to be?"

"On another fancy trip, I suppose," Britt said enviously. "Where is it this time? Hawaii? Paris?"

"No, neither one of those." I considered whether or

not I should tell them; I didn't really want to seriously consider the idea of going to visit Audrey by myself, but on the other hand, it would be nice to get their opinion.

I finally decided to go ahead and run it past them. "I might be going to Minneapolis," I said, not looking at either one of my friends. "It's not for sure yet, but my parents think I should go spend some time alone with her. You know, with *Audrey*."

Sarah raised an eyebrow. "Is that what you want to do?"

I looked at her, surprised to think that she might have picked up on some of my ambivalence. Neither she nor Britt had been anything but positive about Audrey's arrival on the scene.

"I don't know," I admitted, then added truthfully, "I guess the thought of spending time alone with her is kind of, um, scary."

Sarah nodded. "I can understand that," she said, looking serious, and I was momentarily overwhelmed with love for my dear and understanding friend.

"Well, I don't think you should go," declared Britt. She adjusted the heavy load of books she was carrying. "If you miss the Holidazzle dance it'll be another whole year before it comes around again." She looked at me pointedly, as if she couldn't imagine anything more important than attending the Holidazzle dance.

"I already told you, I'm not *going* to the dance," I said with exaggerated patience. "Even if I don't go to Minneapolis that particular weekend."

I shrugged. "I might not go to Minneapolis *at all*. I just brought it up as a possibility, for conversation."

"I don't know, maybe you should go," Sarah said thoughtfully. "It would be a chance to get to know your sister under more natural circumstances than on a family trip.

"Besides," she said, not looking at me. "You need to finish your 'nature versus nurture' paper, and this would be a good chance to get the rest of the information you need."

I wondered if Sarah somehow knew about the notebook, which was still lying under my bed where I'd kicked it. She was right, I had to admit; the only way I could finish the project was to talk to Audrey and ask her questions about herself. I regretted ever choosing the topic, but now it was too late to change. I was stuck.

"Good morning, ladies," a familiar voice said. I turned around to see Charlie Goodall passing by on his way to his next class. He seemed even better looking than I remembered; I'd never noticed the deep dimple in his right cheek before. He had dimples, just like I did! Rather than feeling embarrassed about the day I'd fallen in the hallway, just seeing him made me feel suddenly better, and I gave him a sunny smile. Our eyes met for an instant, and an unexpected shiver traveled down my spine.

When I turned back, my friends were both looking at me with raised eyebrows. "Well, well, well," Britt observed. "Isn't *that* interesting?"

"What?" I responded, sounding defensive even to myself.

Britt grinned maddeningly, and Sarah looked amused too. "Hmm," Britt remarked. "I don't recall any of the cross-country boys taking time to wish us good morning *before*, do you, Sarah?"

Sarah pretended to give the matter deep thought. "Hmm, no, I would have to agree with you there," she agreed finally. "At least not before someone *threw* herself at them a few weeks ago . . . and I mean that literally, of course."

I gave her my best give-me-a-break look. "He was saying it to all of us," I pointed out.

"Yeah, uh . . . I don't think so," Britt said, her eyes merry.

"I don't think so either," Sarah confirmed. "He was looking right at you."

"Well, he absolutely was *not*," I insisted. "I really don't know why you'd think that." My friends didn't miss the fact that the discussion had added color to my cheeks.

"You know," Sarah said thoughtfully, as we began walking down the hall to our next class. "Maybe you should try and get that trip to see your sister out of the way *before* the weekend of the Holidazzle dance."

She gave me a sideways look. "Who knows . . . you might want to be around that weekend after all."

I didn't say anything, but I smiled to myself at the idea that I might still have a chance to go to the Holidazzle dance. Al*right*, I decided. If my parents thought it was so important then maybe it would be better just to get the whole thing over with. I'd force myself to go and visit Audrey, both to satisfy my parents and to finish my psychology project. Hopefully after that I would be able to get back to my *real* life.

23

"I'm just so glad you're doing this," Mom said for the four hundredth time as we waited for my boarding call. Dad had dropped me off at the terminal entrance, and Mom was using her morning break to walk me to my gate and wait with me until my plane took off.

I nodded vaguely, distracted. It had been easy enough telling my parents that I had decided to go visit Audrey after all, but as the weekend grew closer I had started to regret agreeing to the whole thing.

What would we talk about? I wondered. Aside from the questions I had to ask her for my psychology paper, I really didn't want to hear anything more about Audrey's fabulous life. I also had a worry nagging at the back of my mind; was there a chance that Audrey was still upset about the rude comment I'd made just before she and Will left Cancun?

There was nothing I could do about it now, however; the attendant was calling for my flight to begin boarding. I turned to Mom who gave me a quick hug and earnestly told me to, "Have *fun*, sweetie!" in a voice full of hope.

She handed me my backpack, and when they called my row number, I got on line to board. Before I stepped through the doorway leading to the plane, I took a final look back and was immediately sorry I had. Mom was chewing on her thumbnail, something she did when she was very upset or anxious and had no way to get to a cigarette. When she saw me looking at her, Mom quickly acted as if she had just raised her hand to give me a wave goodbye, accompanied by what I knew she hoped was a confident smile. Taking a deep breath, I turned away and proceeded up the ramp to the plane.

The flight from Chicago to Minneapolis was unnervingly brief; less than an hour later the plane touched down in Minnesota and began to taxi toward the terminal. The sky outside my window was November gray, and an involuntary shiver ran through me as we ground to a stop in front of the gate.

Other passengers leapt to their feet to begin rummaging through the overhead compartments for their carry-on luggage, but I stayed in my seat until I could get up without being jostled. Carelessly, as if I had simply flown in for a day of shopping at the Mall of America, I collected my backpack from under the seat in front of me, nodded a pleasant goodbye to the pilot and flight attendants, and disembarked into the Minneapolis airport.

Since no one except passengers were allowed in the gate areas, we'd agreed to meet at baggage claim. I found the carousel where my flight was listed, then stood looking around, still working to maintain my carefree demeanor. Audrey was nowhere to be seen, and after a few minutes, I was beginning to wonder if there possibly had been a miscommunication. Was I perhaps supposed to meet Audrey somewhere else?

Just as I was beginning to lose my calm, cool, and collected façade, Audrey came flying through the automatic doors from outside.

"Oh my God, Josey," she panted, coming to a stumbling halt when she spotted me, "I can't even tell you how sorry I am! Traffic was horrible, and then I could not find a parking place, and I had to run . . ."

She paused to catch her breath. Audrey seemed different than when I'd last seen her in Mexico; there she had invariably been neat and pulled together, in spite of the intense heat. Even on the day I'd seen her crying on the ferry ride from Isla Mujeres, she'd managed to collect herself so completely by the time we docked that I'd ended up wondering whether I'd imagined the whole thing.

Today Audrey was dressed with her usual tidiness in jeans and a sweater, but her face was flushed and strands of her dark ponytail were falling out of their elastic. She looked frazzled as we began making our way back along the concourse toward the terminal exit.

"So, how was your flight?" she asked, still a little breathless.

"Good," I answered. I never know what to say when people ask that. It always seems to me that just the fact that you're standing safely on the ground in front of them suggests that it wasn't a bad flight.

We made the rest of the trip out of the terminal mostly in silence. Navigating through the endless flow of travelers was like swimming upstream against the current; it took concentration to avoid collisions with the other fish. Nevertheless, something between us seemed slightly awkward and unnatural, and it occurred to me suddenly that maybe Audrey's quietness was related to my unfortunate last remark in the Cancun airport.

Great, I thought. I tried to think of a light-hearted comment to break the ice, but nothing came to mind. I felt uncomfortable around Audrey, and now she felt uncomfortable around me . . . this was shaping up to be a *really* fun weekend, wasn't it?

Why did I even agree to come? I wondered. Then I remembered my "nature versus nurture" project. I'd gotten a C on my psychology test, and although I certainly could've done worse, it was still devastating to see that curving, accusing letter on top of the paper instead of the clean, crisp lines of my usual A. Even Mrs. Gasparini had been surprised.

"I'm not sure what happened to you on this test, Josey,"

she'd said, not unkindly. "But I know you can do better than this."

I nodded grimly. I knew I could do better too.

"You'll have to do really well on the final, and also on your final paper," she reminded me. "If you want to end up with a good grade in this class."

Seeing my downhearted expression, she attempted to reassure me. "Don't worry," she said. "I'm sure you'll put your smart little nose to the grindstone and finish the semester with an A."

I wasn't so sure about *that*. At that point the "nature versus nurture" notebook was still under my bed, gathering dust, and just the thought of it brought a flutter to my stomach. But I knew that I had to pull myself together, and the notebook was the last thing I'd put into my backpack before I'd left the house this morning.

Audrey was unlocking the passenger door on her car for me; I was surprised to see that she drove an aging Honda Accord. For some reason, I'd expected her to drive something sportier, and certainly newer. It was freshly washed, however, and the inside was immaculately clean, aside from a stack of books on the front seat.

"Sorry about that," she apologized, bending down to wrestle the pile of books into the back seat. "I've been studying for the licensing exam, so these books go with me *everywhere*."

When she had them transferred to the back, Audrey

turned to regard my backpack. "Is that really all you brought with you?" she asked. "Boy, you travel light!"

"Well, it's just for two nights," I reminded her. She seemed so . . . *nervous*, I thought, and wondered why I'd seen her as so carefree and confident when we were in Mexico.

Audrey nodded. "Okay, then," she said, shutting my door and going around to get in on the driver's side. She turned the key and looked over her shoulder to back out of her parking spot.

"Anything you'd like to do while you're here?" she asked, her eyes searching for the ramp exit.

I shrugged, "Not that I can think of." My past contact with Minneapolis had consisted of brief layovers during trips to other places, so I'd never even left the airport. Consequently, I didn't have much of an idea of what the city had to offer.

Audrey paid the parking attendant and drove out of the ramp, nosing the car onto Interstate 494. Cars whizzed around us as Audrey expertly navigated through the traffic to the center lane.

"Are you hungry?" she asked. "I was thinking maybe we could stop by my apartment to drop off your things and then go get some lunch."

"That's fine," I agreed, wishing I could think of more to say. I watched the exits pass until Audrey turned off onto one labeled "Pilot Knob Road." *What a funny name for a street*, I thought. Britt, Sarah, and I would've had a good laugh about it if they were here.

"My apartment is here in Eagan," Audrey was telling me, "It's a fairly safe suburb and it's also close to the VA Hospital, where I'm doing my internship."

I knew I should ask her some questions about her internship, but my mind was blank. I wondered whether the entire weekend was going to be like this; I certainly hoped not.

We drove on for a couple more blocks, finally turning off on Lone Oak Road.

"There it is," Audrey said, pointing ahead to a towering complex of apartment buildings situated around a small, man-made lake. "That's home for the next twelve months." Her voice sounded a little sad.

"Do you miss Will?" I asked, glad that I'd finally thought of something to say.

Audrey nodded. "Yeah," she sighed. "It's hard to be apart. I have a roommate, but . . . well, you'll see." She gave me a half-smile that made me curious about what she meant.

"That's okay, I've got it," I told her, when she offered to grab my backpack. She shrugged agreeably and loaded her arms with several of the books from the back seat.

"I might as well bring these up then," she said. "No point in having them sliding around back there."

We entered the building through the main security door and took the elevator to the second floor.

"Believe me, I was glad this place had an elevator when Anne and I were hauling boxes up to my place," Audrey remarked as the elevator door slid closed. I smiled and nodded, but my agreeable mood had been slightly spoiled by the resentment that I associated with any memory of Julian's accident.

"Here we are," Audrey proclaimed, stopping in front of a nondescript door marked 223, halfway down the hall. "As Jake would say, '*Mi casa es su casa!*'"

She swung open the door to reveal an apartment that was spacious but barren. A small galley kitchen and an empty dining area flanked the front door, but beyond them stretched a fairly large living room whose furnishings could only be described as "sparse." There was no television or pictures on the wall, and the only thing to sit on was a single nylon lawn chair.

"Kinda bare, I know," Audrey apologized. "My roommate, Tricia, is a struggling law student, and I don't make much money at the VA either. Long story short, we can't afford a couch.

"Besides," she reasoned. "I'm only here for a year, so there's not much point buying a bunch of furniture."

I looked around, still surprised. I had expected Audrey's apartment to be beautiful and filled with the tasteful furniture of a professional woman. Instead, it looked more like it was still waiting for its renters to arrive. I wondered if we'd have to take turns sitting in the lawn chair, or if it would go to me, the guest, by default.

Audrey crossed the living room to peer into her roommate's bedroom. "Tricia's still out, I guess," she informed me. "I'm sure she's at the library; she doesn't have classes on Fridays."

I nodded. Through the partially open door to Tricia's room I'd seen blankets strewn carelessly over an inflatable air mattress, the kind you can buy for three dollars at Thriftymart. *Could that possibly be her bed?* I wondered. Did Audrey sleep on a blow-up air mattress too?

"My bedroom's over here," Audrey said, opening a door on the other side of the living room. To my relief, her room was comfortably furnished with a large futon draped with a flowery blue-and-yellow comforter. I was glad to see that Audrey at least slept in a normal bed.

Aside from the futon, there was a dresser with a mirror and a tall bookcase that was half-filled with books. The remaining space in the bookshelf was filled with framed photographs, including several pictures of the Cancun trip.

Audrey followed my gaze. "Those are great, aren't they?" she said, reaching over to pick up a silver frame displaying a photo of us around the pool in Mexico. She studied the picture for a moment, before handing it to me.

"We all look so relaxed, don't we," she remarked in a tone I couldn't identify. "Anyone walking by would never know what was really going on."

I looked at the photo, before handing it back to her. "Yeah, I guess," I said, but in my head I was wondering what Audrey meant when she said, "what was *really* going on."

She replaced the photo on the shelf next to the others. "I wish I could say I *felt* relaxed," Audrey sighed wistfully.

Before I could respond, she was pointing to another photo, chuckling. "Look at this one," she laughed. "You and Julian were making up that water ballet . . ."

We spent a few more minutes looking over the photos, then decided to go and find someplace to eat. When I asked, Audrey pointed me toward the bathroom that adjoined her bedroom. That was one luxury at least; each bedroom had its own bath.

In the bathroom, I checked out my face in the mirror. In spite of my nerves about the visit, my skin was actually pretty clear, and my eyes looked bright and sparkly in the fluorescent lights. I quickly used the restroom and washed my hands, drying them on the fluffy blue towel that was next to the sink.

"Okay, I'm ready," I said, coming out of the bathroom.

Audrey was hanging up the phone. She gave me a sheepish look. "I was just giving Anne a quick call to let her know you made it. She says she's glad you got here safely and she hopes we have a good time."

"Oh, okay," I said, a little embarrassed, for some reason. I felt like a child with two mothers looking out for me.

We decided to eat at Finnegans, which turned out to be one of those restaurants where they basically have anything you could want. I ordered a Diet Coke and a cheeseburger; Audrey had a Diet Coke and a caesar salad. The waiter brought us our drinks and told us our meals should be out shortly, then departed.

"So, how's school going?" Audrey asked, taking a sip of her drink. "You must have winter finals coming up soon, huh?"

I nodded. "Yeah," I said. "I have a psychology paper to do too."

This was as good an opening as any to bring up the whole "nature versus nurture" project, I decided.

"Really? I always kind of liked writing those things," Audrey said. "At least you usually get to choose a topic that interests you."

"Yeah," I said, feeling suddenly shy. If I told her about the project now, it would seem like I chose the topic "nature versus nurture" because I was interested in *Audrey*. But on the other hand, that pretty much had started out to be the case, hadn't it?

"Tell me about your paper," Audrey was saying. "Maybe I can help you find some of the information you need to write it."

I gave her a sheepish smile. At least she was making this easy on me. I wondered suspiciously whether my Mom had been looking through my room.

"Actually, maybe you *can* be helpful," I conceded. "I started the paper back in October . . . when I first heard about you . . . because, well, everyone was making such a big deal about how alike we were. And I thought, 'Well, we have the same parents, but we were raised in different environments,' and . . ."

". . . nature versus nurture," Audrey finished for me, looking interested. "Great idea! I always thought those twin studies were fascinating."

I couldn't help but be flattered that she liked my idea. "I haven't really worked on it much," I admitted. "I've been kind of, um, busy. But I've pretty much got to finish it before the weekend of the Holidazzle dance . . ."

Audrey raised her eyebrows. "The Holidazzle dance? What's that?"

I explained. "It's just a school dance right before the holiday break. Other schools have them too."

She nodded, remembering. "That's right; we had the Snow Ball. When I was a junior I went with Craig Benson. We started out as friends but ended up dating for awhile before I left for college."

"Yeah . . . well, anyway, the deadline for the psychology project is the Friday before Hollidazzle, so I've got to get it done by then."

Audrey seemed to have momentarily forgotten about the psychology paper. "So," she said, looking interested. "Who are you going to the dance with?"

I cringed, wishing we could change the subject. "Um, well, no one. I mean, I usually go to stuff like that with my best friends, Sarah and Britt, but, well, they both have dates for the dance this year. I don't care; I don't really want to go anyway."

I expected her to argue with me, as Sarah and Britt had, but Audrey nodded and didn't say anything. She picked up her Diet Coke and took a sip.

After a moment I said, "Actually, there is one guy I wouldn't mind going with."

She smiled. "Really? What's he like?"

"His name is Charlie . . . Charlie Goodall," I divulged, surprised that I was admitting this to anyone. I was even more surprised to hear myself babbling on about Charlie Goodall in a way that I'd never done with Britt and Sarah.

"He's really friendly and nice; he has brown eyes and this great dimple. Oh, and he helped me up one day when I tripped in the hall." Briefly I recounted the story of my literal downfall.

Audrey chuckled. "Sounds like he's a really sweet guy," she observed. "So, why don't you ask *him* to the dance?"

My mouth dropped open in horror at the idea.

"Oh my *God*," I blustered, sorry I'd brought the whole thing up. "I could *never* do that! He's a junior, and he's popular and he's on the cross-country team, and he's . . . he's . . . he's a friend of *Brandon Burke*," I finished, my face hot. The very idea of my asking Charlie Goodall to the Holidazzle dance made me sick to my stomach.

"Brandon Burke?" Audrey shrugged. "I don't know who that is, but I can't see where there would be any reason for you not to ask Charlie to the dance. I thought girls could do that sort of thing these days."

To my relief, at that moment the waiter arrived with our meals and the subject was dropped. I lifted the top bun to remove the tomato from my cheeseburger, and noticed that Audrey was busy picking croutons off of her caesar salad.

I wasn't sure if I was going to be able to eat anyway; every time I thought of Audrey's suggestion that I ask Charlie Goodall to the Holidazzle dance, my stomach flipped over. The very idea of my asking Charlie Goodall to the dance was completely absurd . . .

Wasn't it?

24

After lunch Audrey drove me past the Veteran's Hospital where she worked, and then we went back to her apartment. Her roommate, Tricia, still wasn't home, and the apartment seemed chilly and even emptier in the fading daylight. I pictured Audrey coming home alone to her dark apartment each night after spending the day with depressed war veterans.

Audrey was taking off her jacket. "Kinda dismal in here, huh?" she said, reading my mind.

I tried not to look guilty for thinking just that. "Mm, it's not so bad. Do you ever get scared coming home alone?"

Audrey smiled. "No, not really. It's a security building, and if I turn on the television it doesn't seem so quiet."

"Besides," she said. "Tricia should be here any minute, and she's always interesting to have around."

"What do you mean?" I asked. Audrey's comments were making me increasingly curious about her roommate.

Audrey was just opening her mouth to answer when we heard another key turning in the lock and the door swung open.

"Hey, guys!"

A tall blond girl with shoulder-length hair and thick, outdated glasses greeted us cheerily. Her clothing was rumpled and her arms were literally overflowing with books, papers, and other miscellaneous items. Staggering over to the spot where the dining table would have been, had they *owned* a dining room table, she dropped the whole pile onto the floor.

"Whew," Tricia said, reaching up to peel several strands of hair away from her perspiring forehead. "I didn't think I was going to make it the rest of the way from the elevator!"

Audrey gave her a look of exasperation. "I've told you a million times that you've got to get a bookbag, or brief-case, or *something.*"

"Bah, too expensive," Tricia dismissed the idea with a wave of her hand. She turned to smile at me. "I'm Tricia Nuelle, by the way. You must be Audrey's kid sister."

"Uh, yeah," I stammered, a bit overwhelmed by Tricia's chaotic arrival.

"Pleased to meet you," Tricia continued, oblivious. She grinned. "Make yourself at home while you're here and don't mind me. I'll be in my room studying, but you don't have to worry about trying to be quiet. I hyperfocus."

"Oh, okay, thanks," I responded, not exactly sure what she meant.

Tricia selected a thick book from the pile on the floor, and retreated to her room, shutting the door behind her. A few minutes later we heard the sounds of her stereo playing.

"What does 'hyperfocus' mean?" I asked Audrey.

"It means she can shut out everything around her," Audrey translated. "She really can do it, too. She was in her room studying last week and completely forgot about a frozen pizza she'd put in the oven. She didn't even hear the timer go off, and by the time she remembered the pizza, the entire apartment was filled with smoke."

"Holy cow!"

"No kidding," Audrey said. "The *fire department* was here when I got home."

She shook her head. "Thankfully I'd closed my bedroom door before I left, so my stuff didn't get much smoke damage. But the apartment manager was furious; he had to hire a cleaning service to come in and deal with the clean-up!"

That explained the faint, vaguely familiar aroma I'd noticed when we came in. Audrey continued, "Tricia's a great gal, and she must be very smart, but she's so ditzy that sometimes I wonder how she's ever going to make it as a lawyer. Do you want to hear something else funny?"

I nodded, amused.

"Her entire car is covered with dried wax."

I must have looked confused, because Audrey explained. "When Tricia waxed her car, she didn't realize that after you put the wax on, you're supposed to wipe it *off.* So now the whole thing is covered with dried wax. Every time she gets in it she scrapes some away with her fingernail. She says she figures eventually she'll have the whole thing cleaned off."

"Wow," I said. "That's crazy." I didn't want Audrey to see that I knew as little about waxing a car as Tricia did.

"So," said Audrey, changing the subject. "Maybe we should talk about how I can help you with your psychology paper. Or would you rather do something else?"

"Um, maybe we *should* talk about the paper," I agreed reluctantly. I was dreading it, but it was now or never. "I actually brought part of it with me."

"Great. Do you want a glass of Diet Coke?" she offered. "I always work better with Diet Coke."

"Sure." I grinned, relaxing a bit. "I do too. Lots of ice in mine, please."

A few moments later we were settled on the fluffy, flowered comforter in Audrey's room. "Okay," she said. "What have you got so far?"

I pulled my "nature versus nurture" notebook out of my backpack and flipped to the spot where I'd left off. "Well," I said, feeling suddenly shy. "I've worked on the intro, but my main point is that I wanted to compare us on a range of different things. You know; physical traits, mannerisms, likes and dislikes, stuff like that."

Audrey leaned back and pulled the elastic out of her ponytail. Her dark hair spread out over her shoulders, and I could smell her shampoo. "Sounds good," she said. "Have you decided on a specific list of traits you're looking at?"

"Not really," I admitted. "I just kind of made some vague notes . . . um, a long time ago."

Audrey thought for a moment. "I don't want to tell you what how to do your paper," she said finally. "But maybe we should generate a list of specific things you're interested in, and then we can each fill out the list independently. That way we won't be biased by what each other says."

I had to admit that it sounded like a decent plan.

The next two hours flew by as we worked developing a lengthy questionnaire for my paper. Audrey suggested that we include a section in which we described our home life in great detail such as the ages of our parents, number of children in the home, income level, pets, and even whether or not we'd shared a room. We narrowed the section on personality traits to include strength and weaknesses, likes and dislikes, and hobbies and interests.

When we finally finished, we realized we were starving. Audrey phoned in a pizza order, then ran downstairs to the manager's office to photocopy the forms.

A moment after she left, the phone rang. After a few rings, I realized that Tricia was probably not going to hear it in her hyperfocused state, so I picked up the receiver.

"Hello?" I said.

It was Will. "Um, Tricia?" he asked, sounding confused.

"No," I answered. "It's Josey."

"Oh, hi, Josey!" Will sounded pleased. "Audrey mentioned you'd be visiting. Have you recovered from our trip to Mexico yet?"

"Yeah," I told him shyly. "Just about. Um, listen, Audrey just ran downstairs for a minute . . ."

"Oh, okay," he said, seeming content to talk to me while he waited. "So, how's everyone at your house? Audrey said your little brother had a bad accident on his bicycle . . ."

I filled him in on the details of Julian's accident, and he made the appropriate noises of concern.

"And here's the worst part," I told him. "He's going to have to get fake teeth screwed into his gums! Actually screwed in!"

Will chuckled. "Oh, that's not so bad," he assured me. "Did you know that one of my front teeth is fake?"

I was shocked. An image of Will's perfect teeth, so much like Brandon Burke's, popped into my mind. "It is?"

"Yep. When I was eight my brother and I were wrestling around in the family room and I bumped my mouth on the coffee table. Knocked one of my permanent teeth right out. Boy, was my mother mad at us!"

I could hear him smiling through the phone lines.

"Anyway," he continued. "For awhile I had a plastic

retainer that had a false tooth attached to it. It was great for shock value; I could pop my front tooth out whenever I felt like it, just to mess with people!"

I laughed, picturing Will popping his tooth out like a hillbilly.

"Eventually, though, my dentist recommended a more permanent solution," Will said.

"So you can't pop your tooth out anymore?"

He chuckled. "I wouldn't even want to. That talent becomes much less attractive once you get past twelve."

"I suppose so."

We chuckled, and then there was a moment of companionable silence before Will said, "So, I never really got a chance to talk to you in Mexico. What do you think about all of this stuff? Getting a new sister, I mean."

I was trying to think how to answer when Audrey came back in.

"Mission accomplished!" she announced, waving copies of our questionnaire in the air triumphantly.

"Um, Audrey's here now," I said to Will, glad that I didn't have to answer him after all.

"Oh, okay," he answered. "Well, it was nice talking to you, Josey. I'll catch you later."

I said goodbye and handed the phone to Audrey, mouthing "Will" at her. She looked pleased as she took the phone from me and went across the living room to sit in the lawnchair.

"Hi, baby," I heard her say, before I went in the bedroom to begin working on my questionnaire. I wondered whether I'd call someone "baby" someday.

After Audrey was done on the phone, she, too, began filling out her questionnaire. It was nearly midnight by the time we were both finished, and the pizza box contained nothing but a few leftover crusts.

"Done," Audrey said, laying her pencil down. I'd finished a half hour sooner, having gotten an earlier start while Audrey was talking to Will.

"Do you want to compare them now, or should we wait until morning?" I asked.

"Hmm," Audrey considered. "I'm beat, but I'm curious too; how about if we get into our pajamas and then take a look at them? That way we can just set them aside and crash if we get too tired."

"Okay." I grabbed my backpack and went into Audrey's bathroom to get ready for bed. Audrey crossed the empty living room to use Tricia's bathroom to wash up.

I really *was* tired, I realized as I brushed my teeth. It had been an exhausting day, but it occurred to me suddenly that I hadn't felt nervous or uneasy for hours. My parents were right, I admitted to myself, it *was* a good idea for me to come and visit Audrey.

I took out my contacts, washed my face, and put my pajamas on. As I emerged from the bathroom Audrey was entering from the other door, and we stopped, looking at each other in surprise.

Audrey burst out laughing. "Well, maybe we don't

need to read those questionnaires after all," she said, and I nodded. I knew suddenly that my psychology project was going to be even more interesting than I'd hoped, because Audrey and I were wearing the exact same pair of glasses.

25

In the end, we did decide to wait until the next day to compare our "nature versus nurture" surveys. I expected to lie awake for a long time, thinking about all that had happened that day, but before I knew it I was opening my eyes and it was morning.

Audrey was still asleep on the futon next to me, her face relaxed and smooth against her pillow. *She really does look like me*, I acknowledged to myself for the first time. Our coloring was different and my face was narrower, but we had the same eyebrows and the shape of our mouths was nearly identical. I noticed a tiny scar on her right temple and wondered when she'd had the chicken pox. There was so much about each other's lives that we didn't know.

To my embarrassment, Audrey's eyes suddenly opened and she caught me staring at her. I looked away quickly, turning my head from side to side as if I'd just been stretching my neck.

Audrey smiled and rolled over on her back to stretch her arms above her head. "Morning," she yawned. "How did you sleep?"

"Like a rock. I've never slept on a futon before, but it's pretty comfortable."

"Especially when you're totally exhausted," Audrey agreed, smoothing the comforter with her hand.

There was an awkward moment where neither of us said anything. Finally Audrey cleared her throat. "Are you hungry? I could make us some toast," she offered.

"No, thanks." I'd eaten half a pizza the night before.

"Okay. I guess I'll jump in the shower then."

Audrey swung her legs out of bed and grabbed a fresh pair of jeans and a shirt from a clothesbasket near the door. Her bare feet were soundless on the thick carpeting as she crossed to the bathroom; a few minutes later I heard the sound of water starting in the shower.

When Audrey emerged from the bathroom twenty minutes later, her hair still damp, and I noticed that she was wearing the lapis bracelet Mom had bought us each in Mexico.

"That shower felt great," she said. "Sorry I took so long."

"No problem," I told her. I was wishing I'd brought my lapis bracelet too.

"Do you want to do some shopping today?" she offered, "We could check out IKEA."

"Sure, sounds good," I agreed, although I didn't really know what an IKEA was. I grabbed clean clothes out of my backpack and headed for the bathroom.

An hour later I found out that IKEA was an enormous, multi-level store filled with every funky, contemporary household item imaginable.

"When Will and I get married, I want to register here," Audrey said dreamily, fingering a mod-patterned pillowcase.

I nodded agreeably, but my taste was more traditional. "My friend Britt would love this stuff," I told Audrey diplomatically. I pointed toward a sleek leather sofa. "She'd absolutely kill for *that*."

Audrey smiled, and looked at me quizzically. "You're really close with Britt and Sarah, aren't you?"

"Yeah," I nodded. It occurred to me that maybe someday the three of us could come back to Minneapolis together. I realized suddenly that it no longer bothered me to imagine my friends telling me how great they thought Audrey was.

"You're lucky," Audrey was saying wistfully. "I've lost touch with most of my friends from high school. Don't ever let that happen to you guys."

"We won't," I assured her. There was no doubt in my mind that Britt, Sarah, and I would be friends forever.

We walked around for awhile longer, pointing out different interesting things to each other. Finally I got up the courage to ask, "How about your family? Are you close with them?"

Audrey didn't answer immediately, and I saw the same sad look cross her face that I had seen more than once in Mexico.

"It's kind of a difficult situation with my family right now," she said finally. "They . . . they didn't really understand why I wanted to search for my birth mother. And then when I found *all* of you; well, I think it was just too overwhelming for them to deal with."

She trailed off and I turned to look at her.

"What do you mean . . . they're *mad* at you?" I asked. The idea had never occurred to me, but now I realized that in all the time since I'd met Audrey, she had rarely mentioned her parents or siblings. I was embarrassed that I hadn't even thought to ask about them before.

Now she nodded. "Something like that. Actually, I think it's more that they're hurt. They feel like I've betrayed them in some way."

I raised my eyebrows, confused by the idea. It didn't seem to make any sense; but then again, I had never actually considered what it might be like to be Audrey's family, on the other side of things. I'd been too busy worrying about how the situation was affecting my family, and most of all, me. For the first time, I stopped to take a broader look at things, and it occurred to me that Audrey herself was kind of dangling in the middle of two families.

"It's kind of been hard," she sighed. "I've been so happy to be getting to know Anne and David, and you and the boys, but the closer I become to all of you, the more incredibly guilty I feel about how much I'm hurting my parents."

The look on Audrey's face had gone from sadness to one of complete misery, and I spontaneously reached out to touch her arm.

"Listen," I told her honestly. "I don't know exactly what it's like to be in your position. But it seems to me that your parents are being kind of unfair."

Audrey shrugged, looking unhappy. "Josey, I don't want you to think they're bad people," she said earnestly. "They're *wonderful* people, and *wonderful* parents, they really are. I just wish I could make them understand that none of this changes anything. That I love them and that they will *always* be my parents."

"Do you actually think they don't know that?"

"I don't know." She looked at me, and I could see in her eyes how much anguish this situation had caused her.

"If it's any indication," Audrey said. "The last time I tried to talk to my dad about things he told me that all of this was 'like having a death in our family.' Can you believe that?"

I shook my head.

Audrey continued, "It's gotten to the point where I don't dare mention anything about Anne, David, or any of you to my parents. They don't even know about our trip to Mexico; I was terrified the entire time we were there that something would happen to me and my parents would live the rest of their lives knowing that my last act was to deceive them."

Wow, I had no idea. "What about your brother and sisters?" I asked.

Audrey shrugged. "My sisters have tried to be supportive," she told me, "But I can tell they're disapproving. They're not adopted so I don't think they can understand."

"And your brother? Isn't he adopted too?"

She nodded. "Yes. But when I first told my parents about what was happening they were so terribly upset that they asked me not to say anything to my brother about any of this."

"So he doesn't even know?"

She shook her head. "No. He doesn't know."

I digested all of this new information as we continued to walk along the aisles of home furnishings and decorative accessories. The conversation certainly had given me an entirely different perspective on Audrey, and the turmoil that finding us had brought to her life. I could see how much she loved her family, her real family, and how

much it had hurt her to see the pain she had unintentionally caused them.

"Oh, look at these!" Audrey exclaimed, pointing out a
row of glass bud vases hanging on the wall. Each one held
a single silk daisy. "Don't you just love that? It's so . . . unexpected."

I looked at Audrey's face, so much like mine. "Yeah," I
echoed, more to myself than to her. "Not what you would
expect. That's exactly right."

That evening we decided to take our "nature versus nurture" questionnaire with us and review them over dinner. Tricia was invited along, but waved us off.

"I think I'm just going to stay at home and do some reading," she said. "Maybe make a frozen pizza." Audrey shot me a wide-eyed look of terror and I had to fight to keep from laughing.

We decided to go with a Mexican restaurant this time, in honor of our trip to Cancun. "How about Qdoba?" Audrey proposed. "Home of the four-pound burrito."

I'd never eaten there, but I agreed, mostly just to see if she was kidding about the burritos. We drove to the restaurant and got in line to order; Audrey asked for a chicken burrito and I decided on a steak quesadilla.

"Okay," said Audrey, after we'd dug into our meals. She

wiped a couple grains of Spanish rice off of her chin and set down her burrito, which was the size of a small purse. "Let's compare our responses on the questionnaires."

Audrey pulled the big envelope containing our questionnaires out of her bag, and I wiped my greasy fingers on a napkin before clearing a space on the table where we could spread them out.

"I didn't know that your parents were that much older than mine," I said, noting that they were in their fifties.

"Yeah, they tried to have a child for seven years before they decided to adopt," she said. "They were nearly thirty when they got me."

Audrey had written that both of her parents had been teachers when they adopted her, but soon after she arrived her mother quit working to be a stay-at-home mom. *That* was certainly an area where our backgrounds diverged; I couldn't recall a time in my childhood when my mom hadn't worked.

Things really got interesting when we got to the section on "Likes and Dislikes."

"Oh my God!" Audrey exclaimed, "I can't believe that *Harriet the Spy* was your favorite book . . . look, that was my favorite too!"

I was still getting over something else. "Orange is your favorite color too?" I asked her in disbelief. "How many people do you know who like *that* color?"

We discovered that we had many of the same leisure hobbies, including reading, word puzzles, and writing poetry. Audrey, however, enjoyed running and working out in the gym, whereas I had believed for years that physical exercise made me itch. Audrey hated professional sports, while I was a die-hard Chicago Bears fan. "How can you *not* enjoy watching football?" I asked her. She made a *yuck* face.

We'd both stalled a bit when we came to the section on "Personality Traits, Strengths, and Weaknesses."

"I didn't really know what to write," I explained. "I mean, it's hard to know what your own strengths and weakness are or how other people see you."

Audrey nodded in agreement. She regarded me for a moment. "Of course I don't know you that well," she said finally. "But from what I can tell I'd describe you as bright, inquisitive, ambitious, and probably pretty sensitive, right?"

I shrugged, pleased that she thought I was bright.

Audrey smiled. "And you're fun, and have a good sense of humor. Also, you seem open to new experiences."

I was surprised to feel myself blushing. It was unexpectedly embarrassing to have someone saying such nice things about me.

"Okay, now we'd better discuss my weaknesses," I suggested, feeling nervous.

"I don't know," Audrey said, after a moment's consideration. "You'll have to help me out."

I gave it some thought. "Well," I said finally, "I tend to overanalyze things. And maybe I'm kind of pessimistic, because a lot of times I find myself anticipating the worst."

Audrey looked at me strangely. "Wow, that's weird," she said. "I'd probably describe myself exactly the same way. When I was growing up, the rest of my family was always so upbeat; they'd be playing Monopoly and I'd be up in my room, brooding about one thing or another. Kind of like Woody Allen growing up in the Brady Bunch."

I laughed, but I knew what she meant. How many times had my mom found me sitting somewhere, stewing, and told me with a sigh, "The women in our family always *think* too much! Don't give in to it, Josey."

The more we talked, the more excited I became about my "nature versus nurture" project. There was clearly a lot of evidence weighing in on the side of genetics; even more than I'd expected. I was already starting to write the paper in my head.

To my surprise, Audrey's admitted that she, too, had had difficulty identifying her own strengths. She knew, however, that she was organized and driven, and after a bit of discussion we added "bright" and "enjoys problem solving."

"Now for my weaknesses," she said, looking just as nervous as I had been. Neither of us said anything for a minute, and then Audrey spoke, her eyes twinkling.

"Well, someone once told me that I talk too much."

I was instantly mortified. "I-I didn't mean . . ." I stuttered, sounding like Julian in an anxious moment.

Audrey held up her hand to stop me. "It's okay," she

said. "After I thought about it, I eventually realized that you didn't intend to say anything hurtful."

I nodded miserably. "It just popped out that day," I told her. "I felt just awful because I could see that I made you feel bad, and then you had to leave before I could tell you I was sorry."

She sighed. "I know you didn't mean to hurt my feelings. It was just that, well, my heart was full of so many conflicting feelings after spending three days with all of you, and I guess I just let it hit me wrong."

"I could tell that it made you mad," I said, glad we were finally talking about it.

"No, I wasn't mad," Audrey corrected me. "The whole trip was just so much pressure, and I'd tried so *hard* for those three days. Your comment made me feel like I'd failed, because you didn't like me or have any respect for me after all."

I was horrified to hear Audrey admit that my remark really *had* hurt her, even more than I'd suspected.

"I want you to know that I'm very sorry," I told her sincerely. "And I really don't think you talk 'all the time.' You talk . . . well, just the normal amount."

Audrey laughed. "Thanks," she said, "But I probably *was* talking an awful lot on that trip. The truth is, I was really nervous, and when I'm nervous I tend to talk."

I nodded. "Whereas my family's not really big talkers," I said, then felt like I'd stuck my foot in my mouth again.

"I know," Audrey sighed. "I'm more of a quiet person myself, under normal circumstances. Those were just *not* normal circumstances."

We were both quiet for a minute, picking at our food. I screwed up my courage, and mentioned casually, "I saw you crying that day on the ferry."

Audrey looked surprised, and at first she didn't say anything.

"Yeah," she agreed finally. "Well . . . I guess there was just a moment when it all hit me."

She looked down at her half-eaten burrito. "We had just spent our first entire day together and we were on our way back to the main island, and it suddenly occurred to me that by most definitions, you all were my *family*, people whom I had been meant to spend my life with. And yet we were virtually strangers; I didn't know any of you much better than the other passengers on the boat!"

I swallowed hard, realizing it was true.

Audrey sighed. "And then there was *my* family, the family who raised me. I mean, think about it: my parents, sisters, brother, and I really, truly *are* a group of strangers brought to together by fate, or by God, or whatever, to spend our lives together. I think the whole thing just hit me at that moment, and it blew me away. I just felt really overwhelmed, sad, and in a weird way, kind of alone."

I didn't know what to say. I was struck once again by the fact that I had been so absorbed in my own resentful feelings toward Audrey that it had never occurred to me to wonder how it would feel to be in her shoes.

"And now?" I asked finally. "How do you feel now?" I was afraid of what her answer would be.

Audrey smiled. "I'm working on it," she said honestly. "It's just going to take some time for me to kind of . . . rearrange everything in my head. I'm sure it's probably been the same way for you, right?"

Wordlessly, I nodded. It was good to know that Audrey understood that things had been strange for me too, but now I had another question.

"Do you ever regret that you searched and . . . found us?" I asked apprehensively. "Because of all the problems it's caused?"

Audrey smiled, and shook her head. "No," she said emphatically. "Not for a moment."

Suddenly she paused, remembering something.

"Maybe I shouldn't say 'not for a moment,'" she admitted finally. "When I started the search, well . . . I guess I had already decided in my mind what I would find. All my life I'd been working toward becoming a good person, setting high goals and reaching them so that I would be someone my birth mother would be proud of on the day I showed up in her life again. I wanted her to know that she had done the right thing, had entrusted me to good people, and that I understood that she'd meant for me to have a better life than she could give me. I'd always had these fantasies of meeting her once, telling her 'thank you' and, then that would be the end of it. Maybe we'd meet for coffee occasionally, or send letters and Christmas cards . . . but I never imagined anything like what happened.

"When the social worker called and told me the news about all of you, I *did* have some momentary regrets. It felt like . . . like I'd opened Pandora's box and everything had suddenly spun completely out of my control. The scary, complicated reality of the situation was far from the tidy little fantasy I'd dreamt up, and no matter what I did, I would never be able to undo it."

Audrey grinned at me. "I had diarrhea for a whole week," she confided.

I grimaced. "Oh no . . . that must have been awful!"

"No kidding. I couldn't go anywhere!"

"Or maybe you should say you *could* go anywhere," I quipped, and Audrey nodded grimly.

"Do you want to know why I decided to search when I did?"

I nodded. It hadn't occurred to me to ask.

Audrey smiled, looking sheepish. "Up until now, it had never seemed like the right time," she said. "I always had one more goal I wanted to achieve, one more accomplishment I wanted to have on my resume so my birth mother could really know what a good person I'd turned out to be. First it was my college degree, then my master's, then my Ph.D . . . next I was getting married, and I suppose after that it would have seemed like a good idea to wait until I'd had a child or two. It could have gone on forever, really, if it hadn't been for Will."

"Will made you search?"

Audrey chuckled. "He didn't make me search," she said. "He just convinced me that what I was now was enough. He said that he knew she . . . Anne . . . would be proud of me and love me even if I didn't have a college degree, or a career, or a husband. And he said that it would be a shame for me to miss out on one more day of having everyone important to me in my life."

I thought about that, and caught myself feeling glad in the knowledge that Audrey considered me one of the important people in her life.

"Well, should we pack up and head back to my glamorous apartment?" Audrey suggested, raising an eyebrow. "I'd like to try and get back before my hyper-focused roommate puts that pizza in the oven."

We discarded our garbage and leftover food and headed back to the table to get our coats.

"So," I asked Audrey. "Do you still wish sometimes that you could undo things?"

She turned to look at me. "No . . . I can honestly say I never wish that," she said firmly.

I smiled. "Me neither," I said. And I honestly meant it.

27

The next morning it seemed like no time before I had to leave for the airport.

"I can't believe your visit went by this fast," Audrey complained, watching me stuff things into my backpack. I put my notebook in carefully, though, like it was precious.

"I know," I said regretfully. "But I'll come visit again sometime. And anyway," I reminded her, "I've got to get home and work on my psychology paper."

Audrey smiled. "Don't forget to send me a copy when you hand it in."

"I won't," I promised. "I just hope I get a good grade on it. In fact, after that last test I really need an A."

"I'm not worried," Audrey assured me. "It's going to be the best paper anyone hands in."

I certainly hoped she was right.

Our goodbye at the airport was necessarily brief; it made more sense for Audrey to drop me off curbside at the terminal, rather than to try and find a parking space in the crowded lot just so she could walk me to the gate. We hugged goodbye outside of the car and this time I knew that the tears glistening in her eyes had nothing to do with any hurt I might have caused her. Audrey was a weeper, I was finding out.

"Have a good flight, Josey," she said, wiping her eyes and smiling at me affectionately.

I smiled back. "I will. And Audrey . . . thanks a lot. For everything."

"No problem; it was absolutely my pleasure."

I made my way to the gate, weaving through the tides of airport people-traffic. When I arrived at my gate there was still a half hour until boarding, so I checked in and wandered around, browsing through the kiosks and newspaper shops, looking for a magazine to read on the plane.

"Can I help you find something?" the clerk asked.

"Oh, no thanks," I said. "I'm just looking." The magazine section was organized alphabetically: *Allure, Cosmopolitan, Field & Stream, Life, National Geographic, Outdoorsman . . .*

Finally I came to what I was looking for, right behind *Popular Mechanics*.

I took my selection to the till. "Found what you needed, miss?" the clerk asked, turning to ring up my purchase.

"Yep," I answered. "Sure did." I handed her the correct change and she slipped my copy of *Psychology Today* into a bag just as they announced my flight number.

Luckily, I'd been assigned a window seat. I'm a little less likely to get airsick if I can see outside; otherwise, it just feels like I'm trapped in an enclosed, gently rocking capsule. I stowed my backpack underneath the seat ahead of me and buckled myself in.

Just as I was beginning to hope that I had the entire row to myself, a tiny white-haired lady carrying a tapestry knitting bag made her way down the aisle toward the seat next to me.

"Hello." She nodded at me pleasantly. "Do you think that you could help me put my bag in the overhead compartment? It's too heavy for me to lift on my own."

"Sure," I unbuckled my seat belt and stepped out into the aisle. The woman moved out of the way, while I reached up to tuck her knitting bag securely into the bin. I pulled down the overhanging door and fastened it into place with a loud *click*.

"Oh, thank you," my seatmate said gratefully. "On the last plane, I nearly dropped the whole thing on my head!"

I chuckled. "It's heavier than it looks."

"Yes, I know." She leaned down to push her purse under the seat ahead, then settled into her seat beside me.

"Do you live in Chicago?" she asked politely.

"Yes," I answered. "I live in a suburb called Woodridge. How about you?"

"Oh no," she responded. "This is just one leg of my journey. I'm on my way from Montana to visit my daughter and grandchildren in Miami. It's kind of a roundabout way to go, but it was the only route available when I made the reservations."

"Besides," she said happily. "I don't mind a bit. I simply *love* to fly."

"Really?" I asked, surprised. "Most people would say they don't like flying because it makes them nervous."

She smiled comfortably. "I suppose they're worried because it seems impossible that an enormous, heavy object like an airplane can travel through the air without crashing to the ground like a stone."

I shuddered; I'd never thought about it like *that* before.

The woman didn't seem to notice. "The way I look at it," she continued. "Is that it's something that's simply amazing and unexplainable . . . a kind of *miracle* really. Why ruin it by worrying? I'm just going to enjoy it."

She smiled with satisfaction and rested her head against the back of her seat, ready to enjoy the miracle of air travel.

I thought about what she'd said. It was true: living in anticipation of the worst possible outcome could leach the enjoyment from many experiences in life. And in the end, how often did disaster actually occur? It always seemed to happen when you *least* expected it, when you weren't even thinking about the possibility, like with Julian's bike accident.

"Have you been away from home for long?" my seatmate was asking me, making conversation as the flight attendants made their way up and down the aisle in final preparation for takeoff.

"No, not long," I told her. "Just a couple of days."

She smiled, "Ah, a quick trip. Were you visiting a friend?"

I started to nod, then paused. "Actually," I told her. "It wasn't a friend; it was my sister." Saying the words like they were nothing unusual felt a little strange, but not entirely unpleasant.

"Ah, your sister," she echoed. "How wonderful! I had a sister too: she and I were very close before she passed away two years ago. I still think of her and miss her every day."

She turned to look into my eyes with her watery blue ones. "Treasure the time you have with your sister," she advised me. "A lifetime just isn't long enough to spend with the people you love."

As the plane began to taxi down the runway, I thought about the fifteen years of my life that Audrey and I had not even known each other. I thought about the twenty-five years that she'd spent as part of another family, and the fact that, no matter what, she'd always be more a part of that family than of mine.

I knew Audrey and I were sisters of a sort, and would be from here on out. But we'd also been given the opportunity to be friends, maybe even more so than if we'd grown up together.

"You're right," I told the lady next to me. She'd reached down to pull a flowered silk handkerchief from her purse.

"What did you say, dear?" she asked, seeming to have lost track of the conversation.

"Nothing," I answered, shrugging. "I was just talking to myself."

28

Mom and Dad were both there to pick me up at the airport. "Over here, sweetie!" Mom called, swooping in for a big hug. Dad reached to take my backpack.

"Did you have a good time?" he asked, putting his free arm around me as we began heading down the concourse.

I nodded. "Yeah," I told him, smiling. "I really did."

I could feel Mom and Dad exchanging looks over my head. "You were right," I said to Mom. "Audrey's kind of had a hard time adjusting to things too. Her family hasn't been completely supportive."

Mom's face was serious. "I know, Josey; it's been really hard on them. I'm just hoping they'll come around eventually, and realize that our intention isn't to try and replace them in any way. That would be impossible. And Audrey certainly has enough love to share with everyone."

She put her arm around me from the other side and fell into step. We walked along that way down the concourse, me cozily sandwiched in between my parents.

When we got home Julian was in the family room, watching *Viva La Bam*.

He waved, "Hi, Jothey! Did you have fun?"

The dentist had finished removing the jagged remainders of his front teeth earlier in the week, leaving him looking like a six-year-old.

I came into the family room and sank down on the couch. "Yeah," I told him. "I had fun. We worked on my paper for psychology, and I found out a lot about Audrey."

"Cool," he responded, his eyes already back on the TV screen where Bam and his cronies were shooting potato guns at each other.

After watching for a few minutes, I got up. "I'd better go work on my psychology paper," I told him.

"Uh-huh," he said, not taking his eyes off the screen.

Up in my room, I quickly unpacked my clothes and papers, then cleared a space at my desk. I'd been working on my paper for an hour when the phone rang.

It was Sarah.

"So, how was it?" she asked.

I considered. "It was different than I expected. But in a

good way. I actually got a lot of information for my 'nature versus nurture' paper, so I'm writing it up right now."

"Oh, that's terrific," Sarah responded. The relief in her voice told me how worried she'd been about me not finishing my paper. "I just finished mine this morning."

Sarah was writing a biography of Sigmund Freud, and had peppered Britt and me with Freudian trivia for weeks.

"Did you know that Sigmund Freud suffered for years with mouth and throat cancer?" she informed us over lunch one day. "He had so much scar tissue from his surgeries that if he wanted to smoke one of his famous cigars he had to force his mouth open with a *clothespin*."

Needless to say, neither Britt nor I finished our lunches that day.

"I won't keep you on the phone long," Sarah was saying, "I just called to tell you something."

"Really? What?"

My mind was already straying back to the notes I had left spread out on my desk. I would really have to kick it into gear if I wanted to finish my paper by the end of the week.

The name "Charlie Goodall" broke into my thoughts.

"What was that?" I asked, embarrassed that I hadn't been listening.

"I said Britt and I ran into Charlie Goodall in the food court at the mall this weekend," Sarah repeated, sounding peeved that I'd missed her big announcement. "He actually came over to our table and started a conversation!"

"Really?" A few weeks ago such an event would have been unimaginable, but now it was merely surprising. "Who was he there with?"

"BB and Cody," Sarah said. "But they just stayed at their own table and kept eating. And guess what?"

"What?"

She paused deliberately, prolonging the suspense. "He asked about you."

"*Asked* about me? What do you mean, he asked about me?"

Now she had my full attention.

"He asked about you; where you were, what you were doing . . . if you were going to the Holidazzle dance with anyone . . ."

My heart fell into my stomach.

"What?!" I screeched into the phone. This was an unbelievable development.

"Sheesh, don't yell," Sarah scolded, but I could tell she was grinning. "All I can tell you is that after he asked us where you were, he kind of casually brought up the Holidazzle dance, and asked if you were going with anyone."

I held my breath. "So . . . what did you tell him?"

Sarah snorted. "That you weren't going with anyone, you dope. What else would we say?"

"And what did *he* say?"

"He didn't really say anything, actually. Just kind of nodded, like 'Oh.'"

My spirits sagged a bit. Charlie could've just been asking to be polite. "Maybe he was just making conversation," I suggested glumly.

Sarah was clearly disappointed with my underreaction. "Is that all you're going to say?" she demanded. "Boy, you *must* be wrapped up in that psychology project!"

"Of *course* I'm interested to hear that he asked about me," I admitted. "But I'm just not going to hold my breath hoping that he's going to ask me to the dance."

"And anyway," I reminded her, "the dance is next weekend, so if he was going to ask me, it's a little too late, don't you think? I don't even have a dress to wear."

"Don't worry about that," Sarah assured me. "After we talked to him, Britt convinced me that we had to find you a dress, just in case. So we spent the rest of the afternoon running around the mall, looking for the perfect thing. And believe it or not, I think we found it."

"Really?" I was touched by the thought of my two dear friends, frantically searching the stores to find me a Hollidazzle dress.

"Yep, and wait until you see it," Sarah breathed, sounding dreamy. "It's green; the exact same color as your eyes. You'll be completely beautiful in it. We put it on hold at Marshall Fields."

Briefly, I let myself entertain the idea that I might be

going to the Holidazzle dance after all, but a few seconds later reality set in.

"If he wanted to ask me, why would he have waited so long?" I pointed out.

"Maybe because you've been *gone*?" she suggested. "How do you know he didn't try to call while you were in Minneapolis?"

I frowned. My parents had a strict rule about remembering to pass along phone messages. "No," I told her. "I would've gotten the message."

"Well, I don't know," she said. "I guess it is getting kind of close to the dance. Maybe he'll ask you tomorrow."

"Maybe. But if he doesn't, it's alright, really," I assured her. "I truly don't mind sitting this one out."

"But the dress . . . it's so pretty," Sarah said regretfully.

I laughed. "Who are you more worried about here; me or this dress?"

"Oh, well . . . you, of course!" Sarah laughed too.

"Actually, if you feel that strongly about it," I said impulsively. "Maybe I'll just ask *him*."

"What?!" Sarah yelped. "Would you really do that?"

"No," I admitted, then added. "At least I don't think so."

We talked for a few more minutes and then I told Sarah I had to get back to work on my paper, and hung up.

Some scientists think that people behave as they do according to genetic predispositions or animal instincts, I wrote, *This is known as the 'nature' theory of human behavior. Other scientists believe that people think and behave in certain ways because they are taught to do so. This is known as the "nurture" theory of human behavior . . .*

I couldn't really ask Charlie Goodall to the Holidazzle dance, could I?

My mom knocked on my door, making me jump.

"Sorry; I know you're busy working on your paper," she said apologetically. "I was just wondering if you wanted some lunch."

"Nah, I'm not really hungry yet." I told her. Actually, my stomach had been growling for the last hour, but I was on a roll and hated to quit.

"I could bring up a cheese sandwich for you," she offered. At the mention of food, my stomach rumbled extra-loudly, and we both laughed.

"Sure," I agreed. "That would be great."

Mom smiled. "I'll grab some chips too. And a Diet Coke, of course."

"Of course."

She was turning to leave when I said, "Mom?"

"What is it, sweetie?" She turned back, a concerned look on her face.

I smiled. "I just wanted to say, well, thank you for making me go see Audrey by myself. It really *was* a good thing for me to do."

Mom smiled at me, "I'm so glad," she said, and I could tell by her voice she really was. "I suspect that Audrey is going to turn out to be one of the best unexpected surprises in your life. And in mine," she added, and I noticed that I didn't even feel the slightest twinge of annoyance.

After Mom left to go make my sandwich, I sat thinking for a moment. The constant tension that had been resting heavily in my chest for the past six weeks was gone, I realized, and my head felt clearer than it had in a long time. Smiling to myself, I bent over my keyboard.

Increased understanding of the human genome has recently made it clear that both sides are partly right . . .

And as far as asking Charlie Goodall to the dance . . . well, I'd have to think about that one.

29

It wasn't until Tuesday that I finally crossed paths with Charlie Goodall. My paper had taken longer to write than I'd expected, and I'd just come out of Mrs. Gasparini's class after handing it in. It was good, I knew, *really* good, and I didn't want to have to wait until Friday to hand it in.

"This is truly an amazing piece of work, Josette," Mom had said, after reading it. "You've done such a nice job organizing and presenting the material, and I would say that your writing is college-level."

She beamed at me proudly. "Besides which," Mom added, "the case you make for 'nature versus nurture' by describing the characteristics of you and Audrey is *really* interesting."

Dad had pretty much the same opinion, although

more Dadlike, of course. "Good stuff, Josey Posey," he said, putting the paper down. "I always knew you were the brains in this organization."

I beamed at him. "You know what?" I said casually. "I think I've changed my mind again about what I want to study in college."

Dad made a face. "Please don't tell me your friend Sarah has convinced you to become an attorney."

"No," I said, laughing. "Not a lawyer. I . . . I think I'm back to wanting to become a psychologist after all."

Now it was Dad's turn to beam. I was afraid he was going to start in on another speech about how I was so *much like Audrey*, but he didn't.

"That's great, Josey," was all he said. "I think that's a perfect choice for you."

Mrs. Gasparini didn't seem surprised when I handed her my finished paper. "I certainly look forward to reading this, Josey," was all she said.

I looked forward to her reading it too; I might have gotten a C on the last test, but I wanted her to know I could do better.

Walking out of the psychology classroom, I was wrapped in my own thoughts when a familiar voice called out to me from farther down the hall.

"Hey! How's it going?" I turned to see Charlie Good-all coming toward me, looking amazing in his maroon and gray Woodridge Howlers sweatshirt.

"Hi, Charlie," I said, and was surprised to find that,

for the moment at least, I didn't even feel nervous. I shifted my books to the other arm, and continued down the hall to my locker. "What's up?"

Charlie fell into step beside me. "Not much," he answered. "Same old, same old." I was surprised to hear a slight tremble in his voice. Could it be possible that *he* was nervous?

I tried to think of something to say. "So, Sarah and Britt mentioned that they ran into you at the mall."

Charlie looked embarrassed, almost guilty. "Yeah," he responded. "They said that you were visiting your sister or something."

I nodded.

Why don't you just ask him? Audrey had said.

"So, do you have practice today?" I asked Charlie.

He shook his head. "Nah, the season ended last week. Basketball practice starts right before Christmas, though," he added.

We continued down the hallway to my locker, not saying much. Once we were there I spun the combination on my lock self-consciously.

"You know," I said, opening my locker door. "When you mentioned Christmas a minute ago, it reminded me that the Holidazzle dance is coming up next week."

I dropped my books on the floor of my locker, and pretended to be searching for something on an upper shelf so that I didn't have to look at him.

"Yeah," he said from behind me. "In fact, Josey, I wanted to ask you something about that."

My heart skipped a beat. I'd actually started out to ask him to the dance, but hearing him say my name like that had knocked me clear off course.

I couldn't pretend to paw through my locker any longer, so I turned to look at him. His face was as red as mine felt.

"Uh, anyway," he continued uneasily, "Your friends told me that you didn't have a date yet for the dance, and . . ."

I could feel my heart pounding its way out of my chest. "No, I wasn't really planning to go."

"Me neither," Charlie said earnestly. "At least I didn't think I wanted to go, but then, well . . ."

"Maybe we should go together." The words found their way out of my mouth on their own. I wondered if he could tell.

I heard Charlie's voice as if from a great distance, sounding relieved. "Oh, well . . . yeah, sure . . . that's exactly what I was going to say." He treated me to a glimpse of his dimples.

"Great, it's a plan then," I said, showing him mine.

There was a moment of awkward-but-thoroughly enjoyable silence, and then I remembered that Jake was waiting for me.

"Look, I'd better get going," I told him, zipping up my jacket. "My brother's giving me a ride home."

"Okay," Charlie agreed.

I began backing down the hall. "See ya later," I said, lifting my hand in a wave.

"See ya," echoed Charlie said, grinning. He turned and walked rapidly down the hall. I watched him until he'd turned the corner, then hugged myself and gave a little hop of joy. Not only were my best friends and I all going to the Holidazzle dance, but I was going with *Charlie Goodall!*

As I skipped down the hall toward the senior lot where Jake would be waiting for me, I thought about how I could hardly wait to get home and call Britt and Sarah with the good news. Maybe there would be time for Sarah to drive us to the mall after dinner, so that I could pick up the dress my friends had optimistically and lovingly chosen for me.

I checked my watch, and saw that it was 4:00. In an hour or so, I knew, there was another call I wanted to make. Almost as important as calling Britt and Sarah. I wanted to call Minneapolis.

After all, I had to let my sister in on the good news.

Epilogue

I'll bet you're wondering how the Holidazzle dance turned out, and what ended up happening to us all, right? Well, since I'm not one who likes loose ends either, I'll fill you in.

Sarah, Britt, and I had a fabulous time at the dance, and I felt absolutely beautiful in the dress they'd picked out for me. Charlie and I ended up hanging out with my friends and their dates the entire night, and we all danced like maniacs. It was a blast, and I was really glad that I hadn't ended up staying home.

Charlie and I dated for about a year after that, but we decided it made more sense to break up when he went off to college. I hear from him occasionally; he's got a great girlfriend and they're engaged to be married next summer.

Britt and Sarah are still my closest friends, of course.

Britt surprised us all by becoming not only a phlebotomist, but an EMT for the city of Woodridge. She says that it was Julian's bike accident that showed her she had the ability to be calm and effective in a medical emergency. Britt's more beautiful than ever, but she isn't dating anyone. She says she's still looking for her BB.

Sarah finished law school and is a successful public defender in Chicago; I'm still proud to say I was there the day she won her first case, The People vs. Coach Hagen. She and her boyfriend aren't engaged yet; Jake likes to complain that she's married to her job, so what's the point? (And yes, Jake finally realized there are great women north of the border too!)

Me, I followed my dream of becoming a psychologist; I'm in my third year of graduate training right now. I started out thinking that I wanted to go into child psychology, but after being kicked in the shins by one too many kids I decided to switch to geriatric psychology. I absolutely love it; the old people I work with everyday remind me of my seatmate on the plane when I came back from Minneapolis that first time.

Audrey and I talk a couple times a week, and after all these years she really *does* feel like my sister. She and Will got married and live very happily in their IKEA-showroom house in Grand Forks, along with their two cats and my goddaughter, Claudia. They're expecting another baby any day now, which will make my mom and dad very happy grandparents indeed. Audrey's still practicing psychology, and she's taken up another vocation as well; she's started writing.

In fact . . . she wrote this book.

About the Author

Susan Thompson Underdahl is a North Dakota native who likes to believe she does not have any trace of a Midwestern accent. She once had an eight-year friendship with a ghost, and she can occasionally breathe underwater, but not on command. During the weekdays, she is a neuropsychologist specializing in the evaluation and treatment of dementia and brain injury. On evenings and weekends, she is the keeper of one daughter, two sons, and three stepdaughters, in addition to two cats, two dogs, and one husband. On her lunch hours, she writes. *The Other Sister* is her first novel.

Visit her on the web at www.stunderdahl.com.

● ◌ ●

A Conversation with
Susan Thompson Underdahl

Q. What inspired you to write *The Other Sister*?

A. I've always gotten a strong response from people when they hear the story of my rather unusual reunion with my birth-family, and so when I started writing that seemed to be the most obvious story to tell. Since the actual events took place a number of years ago, it was also very interesting to relive the experience again through writing *The Other Sister*, and I found that as a mother myself now, I had a little different perspective.

●◌●

Q. Why do you feel writing the story from Josey's point-of-view was best? Why not Audrey's?

A. That's an interesting question. When I imagined someday writing the story of our reunion, I always assumed I'd write it from my own perspective, or maybe from several different perspectives speaking in turns. When I sat down to write the *The Other Sister*, however, the voice that seemed to want to speak the most was Josey's. Now I have to confess that I always find it mildly annoying when writers say "My characters made me do this or that," but in this case it felt most natural to describe the events from Josey's point of view. Speaking through her character allowed me to show her mixed emotions and her process moving through shock, excitement, confusion, anger, guilt, and finally, acceptance. I think we all had a lot of mixed emotions at that time, but it might have gotten overwhelming to the reader if I'd tried to show what has happening in everyone's heads.

● ⊙ ●

Q. You are a psychologist. Do you think your own adoption helps in your treatment of patients? Has it made you more empathetic, open, understanding?

A. I think that being adopted does help me be more open to the "gray" areas of life in general.

I remember being on a boat ride during our trip to Mexico and having a sudden moment where I was completely overwhelmed with what felt like the complete randomness of life. There I was, surrounded by my "natural" family, the people with whom I was theoretically meant to spend my life, and yet they felt like strangers to me. Meanwhile, my parents and adopted siblings, who by rights I may have never even met under different circumstances, embodied "family" for me.

I also think that being raised by adoptive parents and having the opportunity to later in life meet my biological parents have taught me a lot about concepts that we study in psychology, such as nature versus nurture, bonding, and identity formation.

Q. Do you think adoption has different effects on males vs. females?

A. I don't know the research about gender differences in adoptees, but I would think that the effect on any person would be different based on the circumstances of their adoption. My grandfather was also adopted, and he didn't learn of his adoption until he was around eleven. It came as quite a shock to him, and affected him for the rest of his life, as you may imagine. My own parents were completely open about my adoption from the earliest time I can remember, so it's always been a part of my identity and our family history.

In *The Other Sister*, Josey's brothers had a different reaction to Audrey's arrival than Josey herself. This may, in fact, reflect a gender difference or may be a reflection of the fact that Josey had been the only girl and her position in the family was thereby affected the most. On the other hand, Jake had been the oldest, and this was no longer true, and he didn't seem particularly upset by that.

Q. Do you see writing as therapy?

A. I don't know if I'd call writing "therapy" exactly, but it does bring creative balance to my life. As I mentioned earlier, it may also have been a bit of therapy to be able to re-examine the events on which *The Other Sister* is based from an adult perspective.

Q. Do you have any advice for adopted children and teens? Any advice for someone in Josey or Audrey's position?

A. Adoption is certainly different these days then it was back when I was adopted; there seems to be much more awareness of the dynamics and more willingness to have information about the adopted child exchanged even after the adoption takes place. This kind of openness may certainly affect the issues faced by adoptees and their families, and I'm sure it does. There are also more supportive resources for support and education. An example is the American Adoption Congress, which has regional chapters across the United States, and holds national meetings every year where all members of "the adoption triad" (adoptees, adoptive parents, and birthparents) can learn a lot about the ever-evolving world of adoption.

The main advice I'd give to someone in Josey or Audrey's position is to know that adoption reunions can be unpredictable, complicated and confusing to experience, and that it's very normal to have all sorts of surprising emotions. Nearly twenty years after my own reunion, we're all still sorting things out, but it's gotten much easier and I always remember that I've been lucky enough to spend my life surrounded by wonderful, loving people. If I had to live my life all over again, I wouldn't change a thing about it.